THE AGE OF EXODUS

ALSO BY GAVIN SCOTT AND AVAILABLE FROM TITAN BOOKS

The Age of Treachery
The Age of Olympus
The Age of Exodus

GAVIN SCOTT

THE AGE OF EXODUS

A DUNCAN FORRESTER MYSTERY

TITAN BOOKS

The Age of Exodus
Print edition ISBN: 9781783297849
E-book edition ISBN: 9781783297856

Published by Titan Books
A division of Titan Publishing Group Ltd
144 Southwark Street, London SE1 0UP

First edition: September 2018
10 9 8 7 6 5 4 3 2 1

This is a work of fiction. All incidents and dialogue, and all characters with the exception of some well-known historical figures, are products of the author's imagination and are not to be construed as real. Where real-life historical figures appear, the situations, incidents, and dialogues concerning those persons are entirely fictional and are not intended to depict actual events or to change the entirely fictional nature of the work. In all other respects, any resemblance to actual persons, living or dead, events, or locales is entirely coincidental.

A CIP catalogue record for this title is available from the British Library.

Printed and bound in the UK by CPI Group Ltd.

TO MARLOWE SKYE JACKSON

1

CONVERSATION ON A SUNLIT TOWER

Dr. Duncan Forrester, Fellow in Archaeology at Barnard College, watched as the trap door in the roof of the Lady Tower inched up, and wondered how best to kill the man coming through. Should he let him get halfway out and then slam the door back onto him, sending him stunned down the winding stone stairs before hurling himself down after him, or should he get behind him, put an armlock around his neck, and snap the spinal cord as his instructors had taught him?

For a long moment he gathered his energies together, ready to unleash them with maximum force in either of these strategies – and then made himself remember that he was not in wartime Prague or Bucharest or Hamburg, but in the midst of his beloved Oxford.

His *once* beloved Oxford. Shortly before the trap door began to rise Duncan Forrester had been leaning back against the sun-warmed stone balustrade looking out over the dreaming spires and smiling grimly to himself. The beatific vision which had sustained him through five years of war had failed, for the first time, to bring back peace to his soul.

It was not surprising: there were just too many unsatisfying elements in his life at present – chief among them, of course, the fact that he had lost Sophie Arnfeldt-Laurvig. For this, he knew, he had only himself to blame. The gods had brought him to her in the wilds of Norway and he had robbed himself of her forever in that wretched bar in Salonika.

He had believed he was doing the right thing; well, perhaps he *had* been doing the right thing, but there was little consolation in that. The act of self-denial had left him bereft, and now that he had reunited Sophie with the shell of a man who was her husband, Forrester looked out on a world that seemed to him bleak and pointless.

Nor was this the end of his self-inflicted troubles.

Take Kretzmer, the half-crazed German soldier who had tried to rob him of the Minoan inscriptions which they both hoped would solve the mystery of Linear B. When Forrester finally caught him, not only had he failed to hand Kretzmer over to the proper authorities, he had succumbed to pity, promised to let him work on the inscriptions as his collaborator, and as a final act of folly, brought him to England.

It was for people like Kretzmer, Forrester had now decided, that the saying “no good deed goes unpunished” had been invented. Kretzmer was now installed in a gamekeeper’s cottage near Woodstock, from which he fired sarcastic rebukes in green ink to every suggestion Forrester made for deciphering the stele’s markings. In the course of the process Forrester had become heartily sick not just of Kretzmer but of Linear B itself.

Worse, his recent sojourn in Greece and Crete, far from renewing his delight in the ancient world, had left him utterly out of sympathy with the civilisation which had once been his main source of spiritual healing. When he thought of Greece now, it was not the great philosophers and statesmen who came to mind, but the twisted egos and warped ideologies which were dragging the country inexorably towards civil war.

He had been briefly cheered by the arrival of an offer to give a lecture at the next Columbia Conference of Archaeology in New York, only to find that as a result of the dollar crisis foreign travel was now effectively forbidden to British citizens. As Britain's remaining foreign reserves drained away the bread ration had been cut, beer supplies had been halved, and to reduce tobacco imports the government had officially asked people to "smoke your cigarettes down to the butts". American movies were now too expensive to import, whale meat was being offered as a grim, oily alternative to beef and all over the country there were posters on bombed-out buildings urging people to work harder and longer.

The previous winter had been disastrous, the worst for centuries, blizzards leaving roads blocked by fifteen-foot high snowdrifts, power stations without coal, factories idle, and farmers trying to dig parsnips from the frozen ground with pneumatic drills. And now the weather was mocking the country again, as enervating sunshine dried up the reservoirs and parched the fields and in the sweltering cities, where ice was unobtainable, even the swimming pools were closed because of the polio scare. As tempers frayed, the divorce rate began to soar, and it seemed to Forrester the entire country was on edge.

Then there was his relationship with the newly elected Master of Barnard College.

Dr. Andrew Stephenson was one of Britain's most distinguished metallurgists, a man of the left who had considerable influence with the new Labour government. He had got to know many of the key ministers during the war, when he had helped the novelist C. P. Snow to mobilise Britain's scientific expertise against Hitler.

All these factors had played into the college's decision to elect him, and Forrester knew that politically, and in many ways intellectually, it was the right decision; but he had not been able to establish a real relationship with Stephenson – and Stephenson, perhaps not surprisingly in view of what had happened to his predecessor, seemed reluctant to get close to him.

But it was the stultifying heat that was affecting Forrester the most, even up here on the Lady Tower, and he cast his mind back nostalgically to the pale cool summers of his Humberside childhood.

It was in the midst of this thought that the trapdoor had begun to open and for a brief moment he was no longer a respectable academic in an Oxford college, but his old self, an agent of the Special Operations Executive in occupied Europe.

He forced himself to relax, to remember it was

peacetime and assume this was not an enemy but simply a chance intruder on his sun-drugged solitude. And when the man emerged, silhouetted against the sky, Forrester let out a sigh of relief, because the newcomer had a distinctive army ammunition satchel over his shoulder.

"I thought I'd find you up here," said Ken Harrison, cheerfully.

"Dammit," said Forrester. "I forgot again, didn't I?"

"Don't mention it," said Harrison, settling down on the roof beside him and leaning back comfortably against the balustrade. "I'd rather take my tutorial up here instead of your rooms anyway. If you're up for it, of course. If not I can always just leave my essay behind."

"I'm not so far gone as that," said Forrester. "The Eleusinian Mysteries, if I recall rightly."

The Eleusinian Mysteries were the most sacred initiation rites in ancient Greece, assuring devotees of a place in the afterlife through dramatic re-enactments of the abduction of Persephone by the King of the Underworld, mirroring the annual progress of the seasons. Forrester was fairly certain that these rituals had involved significant quantities of hallucinogenic drugs.

"Yes, the Mysteries," said Harrison, and removed a sheaf of much-amended papers from his ammunition bag. But instead of reading them, he glanced through the contents, pulled a face and hesitated. After a moment Forrester realised that Harrison was embarrassed about something, and given Harrison's general insouciance about his lack of academic brilliance, it probably wasn't the essay.

"Something on your mind?" asked Forrester. Visibly relieved, Harrison put the papers aside.

"Yes," he said. "Frankly, we're worried about you. All of us."

"All of who?"

"All the people you tutor. You're one of the most brilliant people any of us have ever encountered. You're a fantastic teacher and we're enormously lucky to have you. But you haven't been the same since you got back from Greece, and I want to know if there's anything we can do to help."

Forrester stared at him, both touched and appalled at the intrusion; but it was impossible to be angry with as openhearted a soul as Harrison.

"Sadly, no," he said decisively. "There is nothing you can do. I enormously appreciate your concern and take on board the fact that I haven't been showing much enthusiasm lately, which I will strive to correct. But I'm feeling flat, and there is nothing you, I, or anybody else can do about it."

"Flat," said Harrison. "Yes, that's the word. I think half the chaps who've come back from the war are feeling about as lively as a bottle of week-old orangeade. I suppose it's only to be expected. All that saving the world tends to wind the nerves up a bit. And then when it all stops – well, you know as well as I do."

"I do," said Forrester. "It was probably just the Lyall case and what happened in Greece that postponed my reaction."

Shortly after returning to Oxford from the war, Forrester had tried to save a colleague from a conviction for murder after a killing in the college grounds; then, during an archaeological expedition to Greece, he had become embroiled in the run-up to its current civil war.

"There is that," said Harrison, "yes." He paused, uncertainly, and Forrester began to realise that Harrison's expressions of concern about his mental state were actually just his way of working round to what was really on his mind. Forrester waited for a moment before speaking.

"You believe I need something to prevent me sinking further into the Slough of Despond?"

"Well, possibly," said Harrison, reluctantly. "Since you seem to thrive on challenges. But this one may not be entirely inappropriate."

"What may not be entirely inappropriate?"

"What I'm about to tell you. Ask you about. Draw to your attention. It has nothing to do with the Eleusinian Mysteries."

"I'd guessed that," said Forrester.

"On the other hand, like the Mysteries, it does involve the supernatural. Or appears to. Probably not, of course."

"Caveats noted," said Forrester. "Now spit it out, before I throw you off the bloody roof."

"Of course," said Harrison, and proceeded in his customary leisurely way to light his pipe. When it was finally sending out puffs of not unpleasantly scented tobacco, he said, "Have you ever heard of a Sumerian demon called Asag?"

Forrester closed his eyes: he did not claim to have a photographic memory but with a moment's thought he could usually bring to mind any name or concept he had ever read about. He didn't see the page on which he had originally read it, but he could reconstruct the context; it felt like doing a jigsaw puzzle inside his head.

"I think he's mentioned in a Sumerian mythological poem. 'Lugal-e' or something. He was supposed to be a demon so monstrous that if he walked alongside a river the fish swimming in it would be boiled alive. If I recall rightly he was usually accompanied by a troop of rock demons which he had created by making love to a mountain, which sounds like a very uncomfortable thing to do. All in all a fairly disagreeable-sounding fellow."

"Very much so," said Harrison. "And he seems to have it in for a friend of mine."

Forrester raised an eyebrow.

"All right, you've hooked me," he said. "Tell me who your friend is and what a Sumerian demon has got against him."

"His name is Templar," said Harrison, drawing happily on the pipe now. "Charles Templar. We went through Signals school together and then lost touch. I ended up, as you know, at Arnhem; Templar was at El Alamein with Monty. Got blown up by a German landmine, which I think between ourselves affected his nerves somewhat. One day, when he was recovering in Cairo, he came across some chap in a market selling antiquarian bits and pieces, including a cylinder seal the dealer claimed came from Ur of the Chaldees."

Forrester smiled: the phrase took him back to the Hull pier on the edge of the Humber, where he had sat one Saturday afternoon, lulled by the hooting of the ferry and the cries of the seagulls, hypnotised by a book he had just taken out from the Central Library. *Ur of the Chaldees* by

Sir Leonard Woolley, which was an account of the seven years the archaeologist had just spent excavating Tell el-Muqayyar, the Mound of Pitch, halfway between Baghdad and the Persian Gulf, to prove that it was indeed the city described in Genesis as the birthplace of Abraham, founding father of Judaism, Christianity and Islam.

Now the Lord had said unto Abram,
Get thee out of thy country, and from thy kindred,
and from thy father's house,
unto a land that I will shew thee:
And I will make of thee a great nation,
and I will bless thee, and make thy name great;
and thou shalt be a blessing.

He heard the words in his mother's flat Yorkshire voice, as she had read them aloud from the Bible on Sunday evenings, and they still resonated.

"Very shrewd of the dealer," said Forrester. "I'm sure he found Ur of the Chaldees a very good sales pitch."

"It certainly worked on Templar," said Harrison. "He bought the seal and managed to keep it with him all through the war as a sort of talisman."

"Good for him," said Forrester. "And now?"

"Now he's back with the Foreign Office and he's been getting threatening messages about it."

"Threatening messages?"

"In cuneiform."

"Cuneiform?" said Forrester. "Don't tell me

somebody's been sending him clay tablets?"

"Not quite," said Harrison. "Photographs of clay tablets, inscribed with curses in ancient Sumerian, all demanding that he gives up the seal."

"And has Asag explained exactly how your friend is supposed to get the seal back to him?"

"Not yet," said Harrison. "I told Templar he should talk to you."

"Well, he certainly needs to talk to somebody, starting with the police," said Forrester. "But what on earth made you feel I could be of the slightest use to him?"

"Instinct," said Harrison. He puffed his pipe again for a moment. "And the fact that you did pretty well when your friend Gordon Clark was up against it."

Forrester inclined his head in acknowledgement. Both men knew perfectly well that Harrison had volunteered *his* help when Gordon Clark was accused of murder, and that without him Forrester might never have saved him from the gallows. Now one of Harrison's friends was in trouble there was no way Forrester could refuse to at least discuss the case.

"Of course, I'd be perfectly happy to talk to Templar," he said. "But I meant what I said about the police. Has he already been to them?"

"Oh, yes," said Harrison, "and got the kind of dusty answer you might expect. Scotland Yard has many virtues, but an open mind about the supernatural isn't one of them."

"I don't have an open mind about the supernatural either," said Forrester, "and I'm damn sure neither Asag nor any other *utukku* is behind this."

"*Utukku*?" said Harrison.

"Asag was an *utukku*," said Forrester as the facts reassembled themselves, unbidden in his mind. "*Utukkus* were a kind of spirit that had escaped from the Sumerian underworld. They're mentioned in the epic of Gilgamesh."

"You do see, don't you," said Harrison, "why I felt you're exactly the chap Charles needs to talk to?"

"Except there must be at least twenty people in Oxford who know vastly more than I do about Ur. And cylinder seals for that matter."

"I'm sure you're right," said Harrison, "but few of them have your record in dealing with murderers."

Forrester grinned: it was a fair cop.

"All right, I'll talk to him. But I won't be going up to London until next week."

"Not a problem," said Harrison. "Templar's coming up here himself the day after tomorrow with Ernie Bevin."

"The Foreign Secretary?" said Forrester.

"The man himself," said Harrison. "Apparently the Master's persuaded him to come to High Table as part of our rehabilitation, and Templar's part of his entourage."

And for the first time in a long time Forrester smiled with genuine anticipation, because ever since he was a boy, Ernest Bevin, creator of the Transport and General Workers' Union, had been one of his greatest heroes.

2

THE CURSE OF THE CHALDEES

The Foreign Secretary arrived at Barnard College, took in the manicured lawns, glanced up at the ancient buildings – and glowered. To Ernest Bevin an Oxford college was enemy territory.

It was not surprising. Bevin had been born into poverty and for a long time his job had been delivering mineral water from a horse-drawn cart. Then he had joined the union movement and risen, purely on the strength of dynamic personality and organising skill, to become Britain's leading trade unionist. He had been recruited to the coalition government by Churchill to organise Britain's industrial manpower, and for five years had directed the lives of every adult in the kingdom who was not in the armed forces.

Since Labour's landslide victory in the election of 1945, he had been one of the most powerful figures in one of the most activist governments Britain had ever elected, a government which had seized the commanding heights of the economy, nationalised much of British industry, created the National Health Service, and developed the Welfare State. As head of the Foreign Office, Bevin was now responsible for keeping Britain safe in an increasingly uncertain world.

But, despite the heights he had reached, Bevin never forgot that his education had ended at thirteen, and as Forrester watched from his window, he felt a pang of sympathy as the Master of Barnard came out to usher him into the Lodge. It was as much as Forrester could do not to hurry down to greet Bevin himself – but he knew he must wait until the appointed hour.

Ten minutes later there was a knock on his door and Ken Harrison ushered in Charles Templar, a dark-haired, worried-looking man of about thirty. Templar shook Forrester by the hand.

"I'm enormously grateful that you agreed to see me, Dr. Forrester, and in some ways I feel the most frightful fool for bothering you. On one level this is obviously some kind of hoax, but on another it feels deadly serious."

"It's almost certainly both," said Forrester. "The attempt to convince you that there is some sort of supernatural element behind the threat is obviously bogus, but that doesn't mean the threat itself isn't real. Have you any idea who might want this seal badly enough to try to frighten you into handing it over?"

"None at all. Only a few people even know I have it."

"A few? Who, for example?"

"Well, my wife Angela, for a start. And one or two members of the family of course. Other people who were in the service with me. Perhaps some people at work."

"You often mentioned it, then?"

"Not often – but I made no particular secret of it when it came up in conversation."

"Did you show it to people?"

"Only if they asked."

"And had you recently shown it to anyone before these threatening messages started to arrive?"

"I've racked my brains about that, and I'm pretty sure I haven't shown it to anyone for months. In fact I'd mislaid it and only recently found it again."

"Mislaid it where?"

"I finally found it in the back of a drawer in my office desk."

"When you did show it to people, did you just show them the seal itself or did you roll it out to reveal the complete image?"

"Generally the former, but I must admit that once or twice when there was a suitable medium, I would show how it worked."

"Do you have it with you now?"

"I do."

"May I look at it?"

"Of course," said Templar. "I keep it in the box where my wife's engagement ring used to be." He took from his pocket a small leather case bearing the inscription of a Bond Street jewellers.

Forrester opened the box carefully and saw, nestled inside on the silk, a small black cylinder about an inch and a quarter long and a quarter inch in diameter. At first glance it appeared to be entirely blank, and might have been mistaken, Forrester thought, for a small twist of liquorice.

"Obsidian?"

"I believe so."

"Which means it's very hard to make out the markings."

"I can't see any markings at all," said Harrison. Forrester took out a magnifying glass.

"Take a look through this," he said. Harrison took the tiny object between his big fingers and peered at it for a moment.

"All I can see is scratches."

"Scratches containing a vast amount of information, which we can elicit with the aid of this," said Forrester, bringing out the lid of an oblong tin, which had once contained a pound of Needler's Toffee. Upside down, the lid provided a flat surface with a quarter-inch lip all around it into which Forrester, in preparation for this meeting, had packed a small amount of plasticine.

He now took the little cylinder, held it loosely between thumb and forefinger, and rolled it firmly but steadily along the surface of the clay.

"Good Lord," said Harrison, as a complete miniature landscape unfolded before his eyes. "It's an engraving."

"In Sumer people used cylinder seals the way signature rings were used in the Middle Ages," said Forrester. "They were a perfect way of authenticating something that had been written in wet clay, which, as paper hadn't yet been invented, was their chief medium."

"Using cuneiform, of course," said Harrison.

"Exactly," said Forrester. "The Sumerians came up with the idea of cuneiform script and cylinder seals at about the same time. But the seals weren't just for authentication: they were sometimes regarded as magical objects in themselves. Let's look a little closer to see what your one depicts, Mr. Templar."

And he took the magnifying glass back from Harrison and leant close to the little rectangle of indented clay. It was as if, he felt, he was looking through a keyhole directly into the dawn of civilisation.

The cylinder had rolled out an image of an eerie, almost surreal landscape. In stylised form, there were two mountains, each with a tree on it. Between them ran a river teeming with tiny fish. Hovering above the mountains was a winged, goat-like figure, with curious ladder-like markings on its chest, almost like the frogging on a hussar's jacket. Emerging from the river was an equally bizarre creature that seemed to be half man, half bird, with something in its mouth. On closer examination Forrester saw that the object was the head of a man. The artist had even succeeded in giving that grisly trophy an expression of blind terror.

"I think the figure coming out of the river must be Asag," said Templar. "Am I right?"

"I believe so," said Forrester. "The winged goat overhead is almost certainly Narak of the seven seals. The Sumerians were fascinated by the number seven: there were groups of seven gods, seven demons, seven sages. See those indentations in Narak's chest, like the rungs of a ladder? That's where the seals are secreted as he collects them. When he has all seven, according to the mythology, he will hold the fate of the world in his hands. The tree on the left is the tree of life, later to feature, of course, in the story of the Garden of Eden. Note the crescent moon up above: that's a reference to Sin, the moon god."

Harrison had retrieved the magnifying glass again. "I have to say it's a pretty sinister-looking little scene," he said. "You don't get the impression these people felt the gods were there to look after them."

"I quite agree," said Forrester. "The Sumerians feared the great gods rather than loved them, and they feared their demons even more. Which was what the priests intended, of course. What better way to ensure people do what they're told?"

"So, is this seal of mine particularly unusual?" asked Templar. "Is there anything here which would explain why somebody is going to desperate lengths to get hold of it?"

"On one level, no," said Forrester. "These things were produced in great numbers. They were frequently buried with their owners, so they're often found in excavations, and the stone doesn't easily disintegrate, so they tend to survive. If a collector wanted something similar I'm sure he could get hold of it by perfectly legitimate means."

"So why threaten me with a terrible death unless I hand it over?" asked Templar. His tone was light, and there was the ghost of an ironic smile on his face as he spoke, but Forrester knew that, beneath the bravado, the man was afraid.

And though he did not say so, Forrester was certain he had reason to be. He could sense the malice that lay behind this veneer of ancient superstition.

"As I said, cylinder seals were sometimes held to have

magical properties," said Forrester. "That may be the case with this one. It could be that its original owner believed it gave him – or her – the power to cast a spell over a victim."

"Or unleash an *utukku* on him," said Harrison.

"Exactly," said Forrester. "May I see the documents that contain the threats?"

Templar opened his briefcase and took out a buff envelope. He unwound the string that held the clasp closed and withdrew two eight-by-ten black and white photographs of cuneiform tablets, which he laid out on the desk beside the clay.

"Do you have the original envelopes?" said Forrester.

"I do," said Templar, bringing out a folder. "The police have already checked them for fingerprints, but whoever posted them must have been wearing gloves." Forrester opened the folder and examined the envelopes without touching them. The postmarks indicated they had all been sent from different locations, but he noted they were all in central London.

"The address is typed. Did the police see anything distinctive about the typeface?"

"No. They said it was probably done on a Remington Noiseless, as used in a thousand homes and government departments, which doesn't get us very far. Here are the translations I had done." He handed Forrester a set of typed sheets.

"By whom?"

"A pal at the FCO who makes a hobby of these things."

"Name?"

"Crispin Priestley. He's on the Middle East desk."

Forrester cast an eye over the translations to check they had not been typed on the same machine which had been used to address the envelopes, and was satisfied that was not the case.

"By the way, I assume you've reported all this to whoever's in charge of security at King Charles Street?"

"Of course. Toby Lanchester went into it all very thoroughly. Like the police he thinks someone's pulling my leg."

Forrester began to read.

```
The seal thief will be found
The seal thief will be found by Asag
He will come for him in the night
Unless it is given up
```

"This is from the Samana Tablets," said Forrester. "In St. John Townsend's translation, I think."

"Sinjun Townsend?" said Harrison, looking puzzled.

"Spelt St. John," said Forrester. "Pronounced Sinjun. I assume your friend Priestley was using Townsend's text as a guide."

"Possibly; I know he used a book," said Templar. "Priestley's an enthusiast, not an expert."

Forrester laid the typed translation beside the photographs and compared them. Then he nodded and Templar handed him the second typed sheet.

```
He who sleeps on the roof,
Will die on the roof,
He who sleeps in the house,
Will have no burial,
There is no hiding place from Asag
For he who has the seal.
```

"I know it's ridiculous," said Templar, "but I've been wondering whether I didn't bring down some ancient curse on myself when I bought the damned thing. Sumerian magic was quite real to the Sumerians. Who's to say it hasn't lasted five thousand years?"

"Sumerian *belief* in magic was quite real," said Forrester. "The actual magic itself was about as real as a conjuring trick. You know they used water pipes and echo chambers to try and convince people that the statues of the gods actually spoke? They even pretended to feed them, which was why the poor bloody peasants kept having to bring food offerings. The whole thing was a con trick, Templar, and so is this."

"On one level of course I accept that," said Templar. "But in the early hours of the morning, when you're lying there in the dark…" His voice trailed off. Forrester put a hand on his arm.

"Remember that Sumerian demons do not know how to take photographs of ancient cuneiform tablets. This is from someone who knows you and has it in for you, and our task is to work out who that is and make him stop. Or her, of course. You haven't offended any lovers lately, have you? Or stolen any other men's wives?"

"Absolutely not," said Templar firmly. "I've been faithful to Angela since the day we met, and I'd never do anything to hurt her. We married before I was sent to North Africa, and I feel damn grateful she waited for me all those years. Plenty didn't – you know what the theatre's like."

"The theatre?"

"Templar's married to the beautiful Angela Shearer," said Harrison. "The sweetheart of Shaftesbury Avenue."

"You're a lucky man," said Forrester, noting how quickly Templar had pivoted from the possibility of his infidelity to the question of his wife's continued faithfulness.

"What about this chap Priestley? I know you called him in to translate, but have you considered the possibility that he was the one who sent the photographs in the first place?"

"I hadn't," said Templar. "He just saw me looking at the pictures and offered to help."

"He made a good job of scaring the hell out of you," said Harrison. "Might he have planned that all along?"

"I really don't think so," said Templar. "When you meet Crispin, you'll see why: he's a fat little chap who looks like Billy Bunter and wouldn't hurt a fly. Besides, if he'd really wanted the seal he could have swiped it from my desk any time he wanted. Why go to all this trouble?"

"All right, let's put Priestley to one side for the time being and consider other people in your life. Because it *is* somebody in your life, you know, not some imaginary Mesopotamian monster." And for the next half hour Forrester conscientiously created lists of Templar's family, work colleagues, fellow soldiers and acquaintances to try to jog his memory about slights and rivalries, of which there seemed to be remarkably few. In fact, according to Templar, colleagues like Crispin Priestley and his friend Richard Thornham wished him only the best, and his sole complaint about the Foreign Office as a whole was that the messenger service was not all it might be. As for his wife Angela, it seemed she was a paragon among women. Beautiful, loving, and talented, she had waited patiently for him to return from the war and was now eager to put her career on hold and begin a family. Forrester felt a faint touch of envy as he listened, but before he could enquire further the bell in the Lady Tower began to ring and it was time to go over to the Master's Lodge.

3

THIS JAM TASTES FISHY

It was strange to be back in the Lodge again, with its worn, handsome Turkish rugs, carved beams and minstrels' gallery, and Forrester could not prevent himself visualising the scene the previous year when Winters had staged the reading of the Norse saga and David Lyall had died. But if anything the room was more crowded than it had been that night. All the Fellows were there, and the Masters of several other colleges, drawn irresistibly by the fame of Ernest Bevin.

He stood foursquare in the middle of the room, looking as if he had been carved out of a granite boulder over which had been draped a suit created in haste by a distracted tailor. The combination of Bevin's flattish nose and thick glasses gave him an oddly innocent, almost cherubic air, and the West Country burr in his voice was strangely endearing. As Forrester arrived he was in full flow, watched with some pride by his host, the Master, who was clearly imagining the college's prestige rising with every moment Bevin was in the room. Stephenson was a striking contrast to the stocky Bevin: a tall, square-jawed figure born to command, only his thick, dark, bushy eyebrows hinting at what Forrester suspected was the animal ferocity lurking beneath.

"So halfway through the talks Mowlertoff took us to see the Bolshy bally, and there I was with 'im in one of those velvet boxes looking right down on the stage."

It was a moment before Forrester realised that Bevin had been in Moscow in the Christmas of 1945, negotiating with the Soviets, and that because he had a tendency to make short shrift of foreign names he considered too ridiculous to try to pronounce correctly, the Russian foreign minister Molotov had become Mowlertoff.

"Well, the bally went on and on as these things tend to do and to be perfectly honest with you I'd 'ave much rather been in bed with a hot water bottle, but I stuck it out till the end and when the curtain came down we stood up in the box and clapped as if it was the best thing we'd ever seen. But blow me down, when we finally finished clapping *them* all the blooming dancers started clapping *us*. So I took a bit of a bow, and finally they stop clapping. But what does Mowlertoff do? 'E starts clapping them again, and everybody in the theatre joins in, and it goes on for a very long time, and then all the dancers start up clapping us one more time. And so the long night wore on. Finally I'd had enough of it, so I gave 'em the clenched fist salute and that was that. Clem Attlee didn't 'alf give me a bollocking for doing that – 'e said it was beneath the dignity of a British Foreign Secretary – but I reckon if I 'adn't we'd still be there now." Ripples of laughter rang through the room; everyone within earshot knew they were in the presence of an authentic English hero. But not everyone was satisfied with anecdotes.

"I gather you had several meetings with Marshal Stalin himself," said Alan Norton, the bursar who, Forrester knew, was very much a man of the left.

"I did an'all," said Bevin.

"Do you hope to return to the good relations we had with Russia during the war?" asked Norton. "After all, we defeated Hitler together. It would seem a great shame if we became enemies now."

"I couldn't agree with you more," said Bevin. "I'd like us and the Americans and the Russians to work together as the United Nations to keep the peace, and concentrate on getting food into people's mouths and clothes on their backs and roofs over their 'eads all over the world."

"And what's preventing our working with the Soviet Union to achieve that?" persisted Norton. Forrester noted that Stephenson gave the bursar a warning look, but Bevin seemed to have no objection to being pressed.

"The fact that the Russians look at things a bit different from the way we do," he said, "which is not surprising. I've seen with me own eyes the mess the Germans made when they marched into Russia. Twenty million people dead and everything the Soviets had achieved in the last twenty-five years smashed to pieces. But that doesn't excuse what Stalin's been up to ever since we won."

"Up to?" asked Norton.

"Turning democratic countries into communist ones," said Bevin. "Trying it on in Iran. Bullying Turkey. Asking for a big chunk of North Africa, of all places. They're like burglars kicking on doors to see if any of them are unlocked. It's my job to make sure them doors stay firmly closed."

"Yours and the Americans, of course, Foreign Secretary," said Stephenson, ensuring that Norton could not continue his interrogation.

"Well, up to a point," said Bevin. "But not all Americans see things straight yet. They still want to believe the Russians can be bosom buddies. It'll take Truman a while yet to get the country to see just how dangerous Stalin is."

"So you think we'll have to take on the Russians ourselves, Foreign Secretary?" said Gordon Clark. "And chance on another war?" Always highly strung, it was as if Bevin's words had wound the senior tutor up to yet another level of intensity – and the Foreign Secretary, sensing this, put a reassuring hand on Clark's arm.

"Good God no, Dr. Clark," he said. "It's my job to make sure there won't *be* another war. If we can keep Stalin in check until President Truman understands what's going on and backs us up, everything'll be all right. And I think we can – because the Russians don't want to start fighting again any more than we do. They've 'ad a bellyful of it, same as we 'ave."

Forrester could almost feel the tension in the room decrease, and his admiration for this rough-hewn figure, once described as the only British statesman who had begun as a working man and remained one, went up once more. He had first heard about him from his parents, who had told him the story about when there was a judicial enquiry into dock-worker's wages back in the 1920s, and the employers had said it was perfectly possible for a man to do a full day's hard physical work and survive, with his family, on such and such an amount of food.

Ernie Bevin had bought the specified foods, and cooked them, and brought them into court and put the plates on the table as evidence – alongside a single meal that the dock owners had treated themselves to at the Savoy hotel the night before. The contrast was so shaming to the employers that Bevin won the case there and then and had become a national hero for the working classes overnight.

Which he had then consolidated by building Britain's largest trade union.

"He's wonderful, isn't he?" said Templar. "I can't tell you how much scepticism there was in the Foreign Office when he was given the job. At least half the people there were born with a silver spoon in their mouth, and those who didn't go to Eton went to Rugby, and here was this unskilled labourer coming in to replace Sir Anthony Eden. Well, he won us over in about a week. He may not be an intellectual, but by God is he intelligent. He sees through to the heart of the problem in five minutes, comes up with ideas nobody else has ever thought of, and works harder than any man I've ever met."

"Also, he gives us wonderful entertainment," said another voice, and Forrester looked up to see a tall, thin man whose languid, diffident manner and floppy fair hair reminded him of the late film star Leslie Howard. "I was there when he asked a waiter at the Guildhall for a nice glass of newts."

"Thornham loves to tell this story," said Templar. "I think he dines out on it."

"Certainly I do," said Thornham, flicking his hair, "because people always ask what on earth he meant, and I take great pleasure in explaining that he had once read a wine label for Nuits-Saint-Georges, and was convinced newts was the correct pronunciation." Forrester could not help but laugh: there was a self-deprecating twinkle in Thornham's eyes that belied his aristocratic languor.

"I can top that," said a third man, who Forrester knew immediately was Templar's helpful translator, Crispin Priestley: he did indeed look exactly like Billy Bunter. "One night when we were at a state dinner in Russia, Bevin turned to Molotov and pointed to what was on his toast and said, 'This jam tastes fishy.' It was of course the finest Beluga caviar."

There was more laughter, but Templar punched the fat man on the arm and said, "I'm sure you made that up, Priestley, it's too good to be true."

"How can you doubt my word," said Priestley cheerfully, "when the king himself has the best Bevin quote of all? Not a malapropism, but just a perfect summary of the man who, as Templar says, we have come in the last year to love and cherish."

"So what was it," asked Thornham, "that so tickled our monarch?"

Priestley smiled gleefully. "As he so often does, without being aware he's doing it, the Foreign Secretary had said something which demonstrated how astonishingly well informed he is, and His Majesty asked him, bearing in mind that he had finished school at thirteen, how he knew so much. And our Ernie replied, 'I gathered it up, Your Majesty, from the 'edgerows of experience.'"

"That is poetry," said Templar, "pure, natural born English poetry." And as Forrester glanced across the faces of the three officials he saw in each one of them a look of pure affection for their political master. And then Ernest Bevin came towards them with his odd, rolling sailor's gait, and spoke directly to Forrester.

"Are you the man who threw the last Master off the roof?" Bevin was peering up at him through the thick lenses of his spectacles, with Andrew Stephenson behind him, grinning at Forrester's discomfiture.

"I was there when he fell, Mr. Bevin," said Forrester. "And I suppose you could say I was responsible for the fact that he did fall." Bevin glanced over his shoulder at Stephenson.

"You'd better watch your step then, Andrew, or he'll have you going off like the man on the flying trapeze, but without the trapeze." He put his hand on Forrester's upper arm and guided him away from the rest of the crowd, speaking more softly now.

"I'm pleased to meet you, Dr. Forrester. I gather you're from 'ull."

"I am," said Forrester. "Hessle Road."

"Not many people from 'ull in this place. Even fewer from 'essle Road. And even fewer that's done me a good turn."

"I hadn't realised I had," said Forrester.

"Two good turns, really," said Bevin. "You got rid of a traitor from this college, and I 'ate traitors worse than poison, and in Greece you stopped a good man from going wrong. You put a spoke in the communists' wheel and probably saved a fair number of British soldiers' lives. I appreciate that."

"I'm amazed you knew about it," said Forrester.

"Well, that's what diplomatic bags are for," said Bevin. "Reports get passed on, and I read 'em. Well done, young man. You may be 'earing from me again." And with a final pat on Forrester's arm he turned back to the Master and allowed himself to be drawn once again into the throng.

As Forrester watched him being swallowed up he felt as much pride as he had when he received his commission.

The formal dinner at High Table in the Great Hall was a success for all concerned, from the students looking up at the great man from the body of the hall, to the Fellows and guests, who all felt they were part of a historic moment. The fact that Ernest Bevin was here, that he was Foreign Secretary, and that Britain had a Labour government, was extraordinary. And Forrester, like all the ordinary men and women who had fought in the war and worked in the factories for victory, knew that it was their efforts in the past five years that had made it possible. The old power structures based on wealth and privilege had failed to resist Hitler and Mussolini and the working classes had had to do the job themselves. Now those same people wanted their reward and the Labour government was determined to make sure they had it – and nobody symbolised that better than Ernie Bevin. Even if they were doing it on short rations and eating whale meat. But there was no whale meat tonight: despite austerity, the college had pulled out all the stops, and its ancient cellar provided delights which even put Nuits-Saint-Georges in the shade.

Forrester found himself seated next to Crispin Priestley. "Templar has consulted me about these threatening messages he's been getting," he said. "I gather you've helped with the translations."

"Up to a point," said Priestley. "I knew enough to help me identify the passages, and then I cribbed from one of the published versions."

"St. John Townsend's?"

"Well spotted," said Priestley. "What do you think it's all about?"

"Someone is clearly trying to frighten the poor chap out of his wits and get him to hand over this seal. But I've seen the wretched thing, and it doesn't seem particularly valuable. What do you think is behind it?"

"Professional rivalry," said Priestley. "Templar has been doing very well since he came back from the services and he's certain to have put any number of backs up."

"It seems a very roundabout way of trying to do someone down."

"What else would you expect in the Foreign Office?" asked Priestley. He glanced around: Templar was some distance down the table. "And the problem is – he's the nervous type. I think he was affected by what happened to him at El Alamein."

"Is there anyone in particular who might regard him as a threat?"

"Well, Priestley might, or I myself, for that matter," said Thornham. Forrester hadn't realised that the Leslie Howard lookalike was listening. "But hopefully if you know anything about either of us, you'll count us out. I'm as ambitious as the next man, but I'm sure both Priestley and I are confident enough in our abilities not to need to resort to this kind of thing. So Charles has asked for your help?"

"He has," said Forrester.

"Very shrewd of him," said Thornham. "How did he know about you?"

"Through a mutual friend," said Forrester. "But, present company excepted, who else in King Charles Street might have it in for Templar?"

There was a brief moment of hesitation, which in view of the present company Forrester felt might duly be called a diplomatic pause. Then Thornham spoke.

"Did Templar tell you about his wife?"

"The famous Angela Shearer, I understand."

"One of the luminaries of the London stage," said Thornham.

"Extraordinarily popular," said Priestley.

"Am I to read something into that?" said Forrester.

"Good God, no," said Priestley. "It's just that, well – she's been the darling of Drury Lane all the time Templar was off serving king and country."

"You think she's been unfaithful to him?"

"Well," said Thornham, "there have been rumours."

"I'm not quite sure how that would lead to anyone threatening Templar with a Sumerian demon," said Forrester.

"I don't think that's exactly what Thornham is saying," said Priestley. "I think he's pointing out, and I would endorse this, that marital relations between our colleague and his very talented wife are probably fairly complicated."

"You're implying that she may have a lover who feels threatened by Templar now he's come back from the war?"

"It's a possibility, isn't it?" said Thornham.

"Although it's hard to imagine some stage-door Johnny being sophisticated enough to use ancient Sumerian literature to put his rival off his stride," said Forrester. But Priestley downed the last of his port and shook his head.

"The problem is," he said, "the kind of men who are attracted to Angela Shearer aren't *any* stage-door Johnnies. Have you read *Darkness at Noon*?"

Forrester nodded. He had devoured the book between missions in 1942, and like many others had felt the visceral force of Arthur Koestler's disillusionment with communism in his story of an old guard Bolshevik caught up in Stalin's show trials.

"Are you suggesting Koestler is one of Angela's lovers?"

"I'm afraid so," said Priestley.

"Not that Priestley is accusing Koestler of sending threatening photographs of cuneiform tablets to our esteemed colleague," said Thornham.

"Of course not," said Priestley.

"It's just that it's a possibility you shouldn't ignore."

"Thank you," said Forrester. "I'll bear it in mind." But he made a note of the fact that the two diplomats had immediately shifted the conversation from office rivalries to the state of Templar's marriage.

4

THE LIONS OF ASHURNASIRPAL

It was three days later, and Forrester had risen early to work on a paper on income distribution and class structure in sixth-century Athens, read a monograph by Donald Moss at Magdalen on social structures at Mycenae, and go through Kretzmer's latest green-inked missive dismissing all Forrester's suggestions about the monophones of Linear B, and complaining bitterly about the heat.

But hovering in the background, as he worked his way through these tasks, was the face of Sophie Arnfeldt-Laurvig, as if she was sitting quietly on the other side of the room, willing him to meet her gaze. Finally, he permitted himself to close his eyes and picture her, and was immediately overwhelmed. He remembered the feel of her head against his as he held her close to him, and the simultaneous solidity and fragility of her body in his arms, and a pulse of pure unrequited longing ran through him, so intense that for a moment he could not breathe.

He remembered the look she had given him when he told

her what he had done to free her long-lost husband from the Gulag. For a moment her eyes had expressed nothing but sheer disbelief, followed swiftly by pity as she recognised what the decision had cost him.

Because, as Forrester should have known from the beginning, once the poor, broken count had been released from Stalin's clutches, Sophie would have no option but to take him back and care for him, however long ago her love for him had died. And that meant she would have to give up Forrester. She had come to him when she believed her husband was dead. Now he had returned that would be the end of the affair: she was not a woman who could live a lie.

She had written to him since they had parted, matter-of-fact letters describing their return to the estate above the fjord, her efforts to restore the family's fortunes in the wake of the occupation, to revive the district's farms, and to bring her husband back to life. Between the lines Forrester could read the truth: that Sophie was throwing herself into her duties to keep at bay the same pain that threatened to overwhelm him.

With these thoughts running through his head it was almost a relief to turn to the little strip of indented clay and project himself mentally once more into the world as it had been on the banks of the Euphrates River five thousand years ago.

When he had first begun to read about the rise of civilisation between the two rivers, he had thought of early Mesopotamia as Eden, a time before the bloody catalogue of conquest and enslavement had begun to characterise the human story. A time when man had only just discovered how to irrigate the fields and raise enough crops to pay for a life above the subsistence level, when everything was still possible and a mysterious unexplored world lay around them, full of infinite possibilities.

But subsequent study of just how civilisation had arisen there had revised his view, and now, as he looked again at the monstrous creature emerging from the river in the image left by the cylinder seal, and the threatening figure of Narak overhead, he knew that no such bright future ever had a chance: the demons were already there inside people's heads, and oppression and injustice were just about to establish their long rule.

"To think those poor people had three thousand years to wait before the coming of our Lord," said a voice close to him, and Forrester realised with a start that the Reverend Robert Glastonbury, the vicar of St. Mary the Virgin, had slipped unnoticed through the open door into his rooms.

"I'm so sorry," said Glastonbury. "I shouldn't have startled you. But the door was open and you were so absorbed in what you were looking at I couldn't resist finding out what it was. Mesopotamian – am I right?"

Forrester smiled wryly. For all his gentle, unassuming manner, Robert Glastonbury had a sharp mind and a good eye for detail.

"Absolutely right," said Forrester. "Specifically, Sumerian." Glastonbury picked up the magnifying glass and looked at the image of the gods.

"You realise that Abraham himself might have made his

living by making effigies of those gods," he said.

"I did not," said Forrester. "That's not in the Bible, surely?"

"In fact not," said Glastonbury. "But there is a strong Jewish tradition that Abraham was a maker of idols before his realisation that Yahweh was the one true God. You know the Sumerians kept effigies of the gods inside their homes as well as in the temples, and clothed them and fed them and put them to bed just as if they were living creatures? So someone would have had to make those effigies – and what better profession for Abraham before he ultimately decided that none of them were the real thing?"

"I hadn't heard that before," admitted Forrester. "But I sometimes wonder if Yahweh was himself originally one of those Sumerian gods, perhaps the personal household guardian of Abraham's family that he decided to elevate above all the rest. Perhaps that was why he had to leave Ur: for heresy."

"Ever the iconoclast, Duncan," said Glastonbury. "No, I prefer to think that our Creator chose to reveal himself to Abraham as he sat making those effigies, knowing he had found a man of sufficient strength to found a great religion; effectively of course, *three* great religions, for both Christianity and Islam emerged from the chrysalis of Judaism."

"Not that the Jews would regard Judaism as a mere chrysalis," said Forrester.

"Ah, the Jews," said Glastonbury, with real sadness. "How those poor people have suffered."

"And go on suffering, of course," said Forrester, "while governments make up their minds what to do about them."

"Did Mr. Bevin discuss that subject the other night? I gather his visit was quite a success."

"It was, and he didn't. I think the main thing preoccupying him now is making sure we don't find ourselves fighting another war, this time with the Russians."

"God forbid," said Glastonbury. "We've all had enough of that, and no one more so than you. How *are* you, by the way?"

His tone was casual, but as Forrester met those shrewd, kindly eyes, he knew that Glastonbury was aware of the same malaise that had led Ken Harrison to come up to the roof of the Lady Tower.

"At a low ebb," he said frankly.

"I thought so," said Glastonbury. "Would you care to tell me about it?" And to his surprise Forrester found that he did want to tell Glastonbury what had been going on since that night in the Salonikan taverna. When he had finished the vicar sat silent for a while, looking out of the window over the manicured lawns of the college, and the students strolling to and fro in the sunshine.

"There is only one consolation I can offer you," he said at last, "but it is an important one. You did what you felt was the right thing, disregarding the cost to yourself. Ultimately that will bring its own reward, if only in peace of mind."

"I'm not feeling any peace of mind now," said Forrester.

"No, I can see that," said Glastonbury. "But let me assure you it will come. Good deeds bring their own recompense in God's good time." Forrester inclined his head in polite acknowledgement.

"I hope you're right," he said, and smiled. "I notice

you don't urge me to speed up the process by attending divine service."

Glastonbury grinned. "It might help," he said, "and I'm always glad of any increase in my congregation, but I'm afraid I simply can't bring myself to proselytise. It would make me feel like a vacuum cleaner salesman."

"Souls cleansed with the latest methods," said Forrester. "Might make a good sales pitch."

"But not for me," said Glastonbury. "I'm not selling anything, you see, merely offering the product for free. Nevertheless, I do find the words of the Anglican prayer book enormously soothing, and it's possible you may too."

"Even if I find the underlying theology very hard to believe?" said Forrester.

"Especially if you find the underlying theology very hard to believe," said Glastonbury. "Whatever our mental constructs, we all need to keep in touch with the numinous."

"There, my dear vicar," said Forrester, "you and I are in entire agreement."

As he said these words he realised there was a figure hovering in the corridor beyond his still open door. It was Piggot, the college porter.

"Very sorry to disturb you, Dr. Forrester," he said, "but there's been a telephone call for you, from London."

Forrester got up. "I'll come down and take it," he said, but Piggot shook his head.

"I'm afraid they wouldn't wait, sir, but they left a message asking you to call Scotland Yard."

"Scotland Yard?"

"Yes, it seems they'd found the body of someone you know in the British Museum." Forrester felt his stomach contract.

"Did they give a name?" he asked.

"Yes, they did, Dr. Forrester," said Piggot. "They said the deceased is a Mr. Charles Templar."

Forrester took a late morning train to London in a state of shock. His call to Scotland Yard had revealed that Templar's wallet had been found near his body, containing a note with Forrester's name and details. As a result, unsurprisingly, the police were anxious to interview him. He was asked to go straight to the British Museum and make himself known to a certain Detective Inspector Roy Bell.

As he hurried to leave, his shoelace broke. He did not have a spare, so he put on his old army boots, which for some reason had not been returned with the rest of his uniform when he was demobbed. The boots were familiar, and well worn in, but their tread was heavy, and they weren't ideal summer wear.

As he walked from Tottenham Court Road station to the British Museum the boots rang loudly on the hot noonday pavement.

The museum was closed when Forrester arrived and there was a policeman on duty outside the massive entrance doors. In the months since he had last seen the museum some progress had been made in restoring it from its wartime battering, but it was still distinctly rough around the edges, and there was scaffolding everywhere.

Once inside Forrester was aware of an even deeper hush than normal: the public had been kept out and those members of the museum staff he saw seemed to be going about their business like people moving underwater. As a sergeant escorted him towards the Gallery of Near Eastern Antiquities Forrester felt his nerves tighten, and when they reached the gallery itself he found he had to force himself to keep breathing normally.

The sight before him was a heart-stopping one. In the centre of the gallery were the massive statues of Rameses II and his accompanying ministers, gods, goddesses and sphinxes, together with the massive stone fist of the pharaoh that always made Forrester think of Shelley's lines in "Ozymandias". *Look on my works, ye Mighty, and despair!*

But today even the drama of ancient Egypt was totally eclipsed by the bizarre scene in the Assyrian room.

The two massive winged lions of Ashurnasirpal, each twenty feet high and twelve feet in length, guarded the entrance to the gallery. The *lamassu* had been carved for an Assyrian ruler in the ninth century before Christ and were said to embody the strength of lions, the fleetness of birds and the intelligence of men, while their horned helmets proclaimed them as gods. For decades they had gazed with awe-inspiring majesty over the visitors to the museum, bringing with them, by their sheer presence, the pomp and glory of Nineveh and Tyre. They had been moved out of the museum for safety during the war and were clearly in the process of being shifted back into position under their respective archways.

"This is Dr. Forrester, sir," said the sergeant, steering him towards a stocky man in a raincoat who appeared to be in charge; indeed, would probably have been in charge of any situation in which he found himself, so bristling was he with energy and purpose. He stuck his hand out and took Forrester's in a firm grip.

"Detective Inspector Roy Bell. Thank you for coming so soon. Watch that bloody ladder! You'll have the whole thing over in a minute." These last words, shouted out at a volume that would have done credit to a Whitechapel fruit-seller, were directed at the constables who were clambering on the scaffolding around the *lamassu*, attaching a stretcher to a rope and pulley.

"I take it Templar's body is up there," said Forrester, more to extinguish any last vestige of hope than because he thought it could be anything other.

"So we believe," said Bell. "His wallet was on the floor, which was how we got onto you."

"May I ask how he was killed?"

"You may, but we don't know yet and even if we did I wouldn't tell you. I'm not ruling anybody out as a suspect at this stage."

"I know Templar reported the threats to his life to the Yard. Did he also tell you he'd been consulting me about them?"

"Tell me what he told you," said Bell, "and then what you told him."

"Now?"

"Why not now? I can't do anything useful until we've got the poor bugger down. Sergeant Morris will take notes."

So as the grim work went on around the *lamassu*, Forrester handed over the photographs Templar had given him and gave a succinct account of their dealings, at the end of which the detective shook his head in disbelief.

"This seal," said Bell. "What did it look like?"

"It's a small black cylinder of obsidian, about an inch long."

"Was it valuable?"

"Not particularly. They're quite common. Some of them are believed to have magical significance."

"And you're suggesting somebody wanted it badly enough to lure him to the British Museum and kill him for it."

"Not at all. I've no idea why Templar came here."

"You don't think he'd come here to give it to whoever had been sending him those messages?"

"Would you come to the British Museum in the middle of the night to have a chat with somebody who'd been threatening your life?"

"Fair point," said Bell – and pounced. "But how do you know it was the middle of the night?"

"I don't," said Forrester. "But I'm assuming that the murderer didn't chuck him up there when the place was full of visitors, or it would have been on the six o'clock news. So it must have been while the place was closed, and the middle of the night was a figure of speech. When *did* it happen?"

"I don't know yet, and if I did I wouldn't tell you, would I? In fact, I'd very much like to know where you were last night?"

"In my college, at first in Hall and then my rooms.

The college porter can vouch for my not having left. His name's Piggot – you already have the number." Bell turned to the sergeant.

"Check that, would you?" he said.

"Is there any sign of forced entry?" said Forrester as the sergeant hurried away.

"Not that we've found. It was all locked up like the Bank of England till the staff opened it this morning."

"So somebody had a key."

"I had a key," said a thin, piping voice, "as did the deputy keeper." Forrester recognised the speaker, a slight bald man with a fringe of white hair, as Horace Darlington, the keeper of Near Eastern Antiquities.

"And are both keys still with you and your deputy, Dr. Darlington?" said Bell. Darlington held out his hand: the keys lay in his palm. "Then how could either the killer or the victim get in here?"

"Perhaps they came with the visitors yesterday and hid while the museum was locked up," said Darlington impatiently.

"You mean the victim hung around voluntarily until there was a convenient moment for the killer to strike?" said Bell.

Darlington frowned, as if offended by being challenged. "I agree it seems unlikely," he said dismissively.

"Unless it was this Sumerian demon he was terrified of," said the detective. Darlington's face darkened.

"I must object to this talk of the supernatural. The British Museum is a place of science, not some sort of ghost train. I'm surprised at you, Inspector, even considering such nonsense."

"It was a throwaway remark, sir," said Bell. "But it would help if you could give me any suggestions as to how the victim got into such a strange position."

"He must have been thrown up there," said Darlington, as if the answer was obvious.

"Not by an ordinary mortal," said a grey-haired man in a rumpled suit, joining them.

"Ah, Dr. Cronin, glad you could get here," said Bell. He turned to Darlington. "The best forensic man the Yard has."

The police doctor nodded sagely towards the top of the *lamassu*. "As I say, it would take a being of almost superhuman strength to throw a man that high," he said.

"Not you too, Doctor," said Darlington. "Please."

Cronin shrugged and turned to the detective.

"When can I have a look at him?"

"As soon as we've got him down. We're taking our time because we're trying not to do any damage."

"Any *more* damage," said Darlington pettishly.

"I'm assuming that the gallery was already in some disarray when the body was found," said Forrester. "Because of the evacuation." Most of the greatest treasures of the museum had been dispersed across the country during the war, the Elgin Marbles hidden in a disused tunnel at the Aldwych Underground Station, other precious artefacts taken to distant locations like mineshafts in Welsh mountains – precautions which had proved all too justified when the museum was hit by incendiary bombs at the height of the Blitz.

"Of course," said Darlington. "Restoring everything is

a huge task, but we were making good progress, until this. Has the poor man's wife been told what's happened?"

"We've been leaving messages for her all over the place," said Bell, "but she seems to have been off for a drive in the country."

"It's Angela Shearer, isn't it?" said Forrester.

Bell groaned. "Don't remind me," he said.

"You've got something against the acting profession?"

"Not in itself," said Bell, "but with Angela Shearer involved the headline writers are going to have a field day."

"Hey up," said a voice from the top of the winged lion. "Lower away." And with infinite care the policeman at the top of the ladder slid the stretcher holding the body of Charles Templar off the top of the monument. The ropes went taut as they took the weight. Steadied by several hands, the stretcher was lowered to the ground, and as it settled onto the marble floor, the body was visible for all to see.

There was blood coming out of the corner of Charles Templar's mouth, but that was not what drew their attention.

What drew their attention was the fact that his chest looked as if it had been crushed in a massive vice.

"Good God," said Bell, under his breath. But his reaction was eclipsed by that of the latest arrival in the gallery, who, on seeing the body, let out a scream that would have filled an auditorium.

As Forrester turned towards the sound he found himself staring at a woman whose white, horrified face was still heart-stoppingly beautiful.

"Oh, Christ," hissed Bell. "Who let her in here?"

Then the woman began to topple over and Forrester caught her just before she hit the floor.

"Don't tell me this is his wife?" he said.

"It most certainly is," said Bell. "Who the hell was on the door?" Then, without waiting for an answer, he turned to a constable. "Get her out of here. Get her back home. Call the Yard and ask for a policewoman." But before the constable could reply the sergeant hurried into the room.

"You need to get to the Yard straightaway, sir," he said. "It's a General Alert: everybody back to Whitehall."

"What the hell is going on?" demanded Bell. Forrester saw the sergeant's tongue run over dry lips before he replied.

"It's the Foreign Secretary, sir: Mr. Bevin. He's been assassinated."

5

ARTHUR AND ANGELA

Half an hour later a police car had dropped Angela Shearer off with Forrester at her flat in Drayton Gardens, largely because there had been no one else to look after her.

"I'll send a policewoman round," Bell had said, "but don't hold your breath. Call me if there's a problem."

Forrester extracted the keys from the actress's handbag, helped her through the front door, and together they took the lift to her flat. All the time she said nothing, staring straight ahead in a state of shock, leaning heavily on him as if she would collapse the minute he let go.

The flat was light, airy and elegantly furnished, and to Forrester's relief, when he had sat the woman down on the couch, he saw it had a relatively well-stocked drinks cabinet. He poured a generous tumbler full of brandy and returned to the couch, where he got as much of the liquor into her as he could. To his relief the brandy seemed to revive her, and then, as the immediate shock passed and the reality hit her, she began to sob, great racking gulps so powerful it seemed they would break her apart. She buried her face in Forrester's chest and he let her stay there, murmuring vague words of comfort. Finally she stopped weeping, wiped her face, sat up and looked at him curiously.

"I'm sorry," she said, "but who *are* you?"

Forrester explained, and at the mention of her husband Angela began to weep again, but this time more gently, as if the wave of grief that had overwhelmed her moments before was receding into some distant sea. Finally she was able to speak again.

"He was supposed to pick me up at the theatre," she said, "but he never did. He loved coming to get me after the shows, you know – and now he never will again."

"What did you do when he didn't turn up?" said Forrester.

There was a momentary panic in Angela's eyes, and then she shrugged. "There was a party down in Henley afterwards, I went on to that."

"Did you leave a note for him to let him know?"

"I must have done. I'm sure I did."

"Did you ever send him notes here, telling him not to come and pick you up for some reason or other?"

"Sometimes," said Angela. "Does it matter?"

"It may not," said Forrester. "I was just trying to work out how it was he came to be at the British Museum in the first place."

Angela reached up to her tear-stained face. "Would you fetch me my handbag please?" and when Forrester did she opened it, used a handkerchief to wipe away the tears and then took out a compact and began to repair the damage to her make-up. When she looked at Forrester again, although her eyes were still red, her voice was steady.

"It's very kind of you to bring me home," she said. "What happened to the police?"

They turned on the radio then, and Forrester let out a long sigh of relief when the BBC news reported that although there had been an assassination attempt on the Foreign Secretary he had escaped unscathed.

"I don't understand," said Angela Shearer. "Who would want to kill Ernie Bevin?"

"I don't know," said Forrester. "The Russians?"

"The Russians?" said Angela, but before Forrester could elaborate there was the sound of a key in the lock and a third person entered the flat.

He was a short, strongly built man with thick black hair combed back from his forehead and held in place with generous quantities of hair cream. He had full, sensuous lips and a delicate chin and his eyes blazed with alarming energy. He looked furiously at Forrester and said, "Who the hell are you?" in an accent so harshly Teutonic it reminded Forrester of a hacksaw.

"The police sent him to look after me," said Angela. "Charles has been murdered."

"Murdered?" said the man. "What for?"

"We don't know, Mr. Koestler," said Forrester, standing up. "It happened at the British Museum." He held out his hand. "My name is Duncan Forrester. Shortly before he was killed Charles came to me for advice and the police asked me to bring Angela home from the murder scene."

"How do you know who I am?" said Koestler suspiciously.

"I have a copy of *Darkness at Noon*," said Forrester, "and in any other circumstances it would be a great pleasure to meet you."

"Of course," said Koestler. He walked over to the drinks cabinet and poured himself a large whiskey. Only then did he come back to the couch, sit down beside Angela and take her hand.

"Well," he said, pronouncing the word as if it began with a V, "this is a terrible thing at this moment, my dear, but you will get over it."

"I will never get over it," said Angela, and the line was so beautifully delivered Forrester might almost have believed it had been rehearsed. "Charles was my life." Koestler took a deep drink of the whiskey.

"How can you say that?" he asked brutally. "You hardly saw the fellow during the war, and you told me yourself he was, how did you put it, *frightfully dull*."

"I never said anything of the kind," said Angela. "I loved him to distraction."

"You loved *me* to distraction too," said Koestler. "Or so you said."

"I did until I discovered how many other women you were making love to," said Angela. "Then I realised you were a bastard."

"And then you loved me even more," said Koestler, "because all women like bastards."

Forrester, by now acutely embarrassed, jumped in.

"Miss Shearer, now you've got someone with you, perhaps this is a good time for me to go."

Abruptly, she took his hand.

"No, please stay," she said. "Arthur is just going." Koestler remained firmly on the couch.

"No, I am not going," he said, stubbornly. "You had promised to see me today and I will not let you break your promise."

"Arthur," said the actress, "can't you see this is no time for that sort of thing? My husband has just been murdered."

"Then I will comfort you," said Koestler, "and this man will go away."

"I don't want him to go away. I want him to stay and look after me. You don't care about anybody except yourself."

"Apart from the human race," said Koestler. "I care about the future of the human race and all you care about is if your reviews are good."

"At least they *are* good," said Angela. "What was it that George said about your play? 'Koestler's latest shows the difference between having a good idea and creating good drama.'"

"Orwell is a fool. I told him to his face it was a bloody awful review," said Koestler resentfully.

"And he said that was because it was a bloody awful play," replied Angela swiftly – at which Koestler rose angrily to his feet. Angela took refuge by moving uncomfortably close to Forrester, who said the first thing that came into his head to try to calm the situation down.

"I saw the play," he said quickly, "and liked it very

much." The first part was true. He had seen *Twilight Bar*, which involved aliens and long discussions about world peace, but he had found it wordy and unconvincing. "And I've been an admirer of yours since I first read *Darkness*."

"What about *Arrival and Departure*?" demanded Koestler, not yet ready to be mollified. "Did you read that, if you like my work so much?"

"I did," said Forrester. "I was hoping all along that the hero would join the SOE, and I was very pleased when he did. That was my outfit, you see." Even as he said those words he was despising himself – why was he trying to placate this monstrously egotistical man instead of comforting a woman who had just lost her husband? Well, partly because Koestler was one of Europe's foremost intellectuals, and partly because he had lived one of the most extraordinary lives Forrester had ever heard of.

Born in Budapest, he went to university in Vienna, and then emigrated to Palestine to work on a kibbutz. Thrown out when it became clear he had no interest in manual labour, after months of destitution, he began his climb to fame by getting a job as a Middle East correspondent for a group of Berlin-based newspapers. He flew with the airship *Graf Zeppelin* on its epoch-making flight to the North Pole, disappeared into Central Asia to find out how communism was affecting the Muslims of the steppes, joined the Communist Party, became a prominent anti-Fascist, married a fellow party member and in 1936 went to report on the civil war in Spain. Where he was captured by the fascists and sentenced to be shot by a firing squad.

Incredibly, just before he was offered his last cigarette, Franco agreed to exchange him for the wife of a famous fascist fighter pilot. Koestler returned to France, left the Communist Party (disillusioned by what he had seen in Spain) and began an affair with a British sculptor called Daphne Hardy. Here he began his first novel, *A Matter of Circumstances*, which Daphne typed in their tiny Paris apartment.

Then came the outbreak of war, and Koestler was arrested by the French government and sent to an internment camp. Again, people lobbied for him to be freed, but by this time the Germans had invaded and as soon as he was released he was on the run. He managed to reach Marseille, joined the French Foreign Legion and was sent to North Africa. Here he deserted, entered the kind of limbo depicted in *Casablanca*, and finally reached Lisbon – where he heard that the ship from Bordeaux on which Daphne Hardy was travelling with the manuscript of *A Matter of Circumstances* had been sunk. Despairing, he bought a packet of suicide pills from a fellow exile and swallowed them all.

But when against all odds the pills failed to work he found a way out of Portugal into Britain – where he was imprisoned once more, this time as an illegal alien.

Only to be freed after it turned out Daphne Hardy had survived the sinking of her ship, saved the manuscript of *A Matter of Circumstances* and persuaded Jonathan Cape to publish it under a new title she had come up with, *Darkness at Noon*.

He was then hired by the Ministry of Information to produce scripts for propaganda films, while in his spare time writing the essays which first alerted the world to the true nature of Nazi atrocities.

In December 1944 he travelled to Palestine as a reporter for *The Times* and tried to persuade Menachem Begin, head of the Irgun terrorist organisation, to stop killing British soldiers.

"You SOE people did good work during the war," said Koestler. "I admired your courage. Unfortunately some of your methods are now being used against you."

"You mean in Palestine?" said Forrester.

"And possibly here in Britain," said Koestler. "You heard what happened today to Mr. Bevin?"

"Yes," said Forrester.

"They say a young man on a motorbike drove out in front of his car and began shooting," said Koestler. "Bevin was very lucky not to be killed."

"Could it have been the same people who killed poor Charles?" said Angela. "After all, he worked for Mr. Bevin."

"The people who tried to kill Ernest Bevin are almost certainly Jews like me," said Koestler, "and they did it because of Bevin's policies on Palestine. I don't approve of their actions, but I can understand them. Your husband's murder sounds more like some kind of personal revenge."

"Revenge for what?" said Angela.

"I can't say," said Koestler dismissively. "What about your other lovers? Had your husband horsewhipped any of them? It's the sort of thing an English gentleman might do, isn't it? An old-fashioned English gentleman."

"You are a pig," said Angela furiously. "How can you even say such a thing?"

"Because I know your nature," said Koestler. "What about Jack Casement? He's perfectly capable of killing anyone who gets in his way." Forrester blinked: Casement was one of Britain's most successful industrialists, an aviation hero and friend of Winston Churchill.

"Jack would never hurt a fly," said Angela firmly. "And he had no reason to kill Charles. If anything, Charles had every motivation to try and kill Jack. Not that he would. Charles wouldn't have hurt a fly either." And with that she began to cry again. Koestler met Forrester's eye, making it clear he was completely unmoved by his mistress's tears. Then he got up, took Forrester by the arm and led him over to the drinks cabinet, where he poured himself another whiskey.

"Tell me more about how her husband met his death."

Forrester hesitated, his dislike of the man's behaviour fighting with the fact that his energy made him almost impossible to resist. Briefly, he explained exactly what had happened to Charles Templar. Koestler nodded, as though the details confirmed what he had already assumed.

"Have you any explanation for how he died? I am struck by the fact that even the police, you say, acknowledge that it would have taken a superhuman force to fling the poor fellow on top of that Assyrian idol. Do you think this is some sort of supernatural event?"

"It's very hard to imagine a Sumerian demon taking photographs of cuneiform tablets and sending them through the post to his intended victim."

"Indeed, ridiculous," said Koestler, "but what if this was the work of someone *possessed* by a Sumerian demon?"

Forrester pursed his lips. He didn't believe in possession, but Koestler had given him an idea. Even as it formulated itself in his mind, the doorbell rang and when he opened it, there, finally, was the promised policewoman. It was with some relief that he led her over to the couch, offered Angela any assistance she might need and took his leave.

He was now very keen to get to a certain Charing Cross Road bookshop as soon as possible.

6

THE GREAT BEAST

As Forrester left Angela Shearer's apartment, twenty feet along the carpeted hallway the lift doors opened and Sir Jack Casement stepped out, smiling to himself. As he saw Forrester closing the apartment door, his smile vanished.

Forrester had been hearing stories about Jack Casement since he was a boy. How he had made his name as a fighter ace during the first war, barnstormed around Britain with a flying circus in the 1920s, survived numerous crashes, been a test pilot for De Havilland, gone into manufacturing, and saved the aviation industry during the Depression. How he had kept engineers and draughtsmen off the dole at his own expense when the government refused to buy the planes he knew would all too soon be needed for Britain's defence. How after 1940 he and Ernest Bevin had worked hand in hand to draft and train the labour force that Britain's factories needed for total war.

And how his famously terrifying temper had bent investors, boards of directors, and the government bureaucrats to his will for thirty years.

Now, as Casement strode towards him down the corridor, Forrester could understand why. The man was impeccably dressed, his suit perfectly tailored to show off his broad shoulders, and though he was now in his early fifties he carried himself like a prize-fighter.

"Name?" he snapped as he neared Forrester, and as Forrester hesitated he thrust his face at him. "Come on, who the hell are you?"

Forrester looked him in the eye and told him succinctly who he was and why he was there. He could almost see the calculations going on behind Casement's grey eyes as the man took in the information, filed it away for later verification, and decided that Forrester was not a rival lover. Which meant, of course, he had to present his own presence here in the most favourable light.

"I came as soon as I could," he said briefly. "The poor kid must be in a hell of a state."

"She was," said Forrester. "I think the first shock has passed now, and there's a policewoman with her. How did you find out what happened?"

Casement smiled. "There are plenty of people who owe me favours," he said and reached for the door. Forrester knew he had to act.

"I wouldn't go in there now—" he began.

Casement cut him off angrily.

"Why on earth not? She needs me."

"Koestler is there too."

"What?"

"He arrived about half an hour ago."

"Arthur Koestler?"

"Yes."

"That damned communist?"

"I think he left the party some time ago," said Forrester firmly.

"I don't believe it."

"If you read his books it's perfectly clear. *Darkness at Noon*, *The Yogi and the Commissar*—"

"I don't give a shit about whether he's still a communist, but if he's hanging round Angela I'm going to tear his bloody head off." And again he tried, in vain, to get at the door.

"Well, you'll have to do it another time, Sir Jack. Her husband's just been killed and I'm not going to let you throw a tantrum in front of her, much less start a fight with another man."

This time when Casement's eyes met Forrester's, they glinted with red rage, and Forrester recognised, as he had many times behind enemy lines, the face of someone who would gladly kill him. He knew too that he had the advantage over Casement, because he had his anger under control.

"Here's what we're going to do," he said. "We're going to walk back to the lift together, go down to the ground floor, turn right out of the front door and walk one hundred yards down the road to The Prince of Bohemia, where I am going to buy you a large whiskey, and when you have finished it we will discuss the best thing for you to do next. Because I'm telling you now that having a fight with me outside Angela Shearer's flat or having a fight with Arthur

Koestler inside her flat will not do any of us any good. What do you say?"

There was a pause as Casement regained control of himself.

"I haven't been in The Prince of Bohemia for years," he said at last.

As they walked down the hallway towards the lift Forrester felt the tension draining out of the man and as the metal doors clanged to behind them the industrialist let out a long breath.

"There's no fool like an old fool, is there?" he asked.

"She's a very beautiful woman," said Forrester, "and you're hardly an old man."

"Old enough to know better," said Casement. "And old enough to know I'm not the only one."

"Do you think her husband knew?" said Forrester. "About her carrying on?"

"What a wonderful old-fashioned phrase," said Casement. "Carrying on. Do I take that as an implied rebuke?"

"Take it as you will," said Forrester. "I've always felt for chaps who came back from fighting overseas only to find other men had been with their wives."

There was a sudden silence in the tiny confines of the lift cage and Forrester felt a brief regret that he had not pressed the button to descend as soon as they had entered.

"Fair point," said Casement at last, "though in this case I think the fact that she's an actress has to be taken into consideration."

"In that actresses are by definition loose women?" said Forrester lightly.

"No, in that she lives in a different moral universe from ordinary mortals."

"Really?" said Forrester.

"And besides, the marriage had been over for years, except in name."

"She told you that, did she?"

"Yes, she did as a matter of fact," said Casement. "Not that it's any business of yours."

"Fair enough," said Forrester, "although it doesn't answer my question as to whether her husband knew."

"It doesn't, does it?" said Casement, and turned around awkwardly to press the button that sent the lift gliding smoothly down to the ground floor.

Here, to his relief and probably to Casement's, Forrester's suggestion that they have a drink together while the industrialist calmed down became redundant. As the lift reached the ground floor they saw through the glass of the main doors half a dozen men in raincoats, several of them carrying cameras, peering at the names on the doorbells.

"All right," said Casement decisively. "You can do me a favour, Forrester. I've no desire to be seen by the gentlemen of the press, and I'd appreciate it if you could stall them while I nip out the back entrance."

And without waiting for Forrester's agreement he disappeared into the shadows of the hallway. Forrester waited for a moment, slipped through the front door, shut it firmly behind him before any of the journalists could push past into the building, and allowed himself to be swamped by demands to reveal which apartment belonged to Angela

Shearer. He kept them busy for a few moments pretending not to know who Angela Shearer was, and finally suggested she probably lived in the mansion block across the road, before hurrying down the steps – realising, for the first time, the priceless value of anonymity.

Forrester then made his way east, by bus and Tube, finally emerging into the daylight at Leicester Square Station on Charing Cross Road. The road was home to some of the ugliest structures in London, but the second-hand bookshops below those buildings were some of Forrester's favourite places in London. Even without going inside – there were always plenty of browsers going through the boxes on tables set out on the pavement in search of a neglected treasure – one could spend a pleasant half hour distracted from the cares and pressures of the city. The heart of the Charing Cross Road book business, however, was not on Charing Cross itself, but a narrow paved alley called Cecil Court which ran eastwards to St. Martin's Lane and had originally been created by Queen Elizabeth's spymaster, Robert Cecil.

Perhaps inspired by its clandestine origins, from its earliest days Cecil Court had a distinctly raffish reputation. Snuff shop owners augmented their incomes by selling Jacobite tracts and books with titillating titles like *A Voyage to the Isles of Love* and *Satan's Harvest Home*, and soon the Old Bailey was sentencing arsonists, highwaymen and forgers whose arrests had taken place in Cecil Court. Then Freemasons and atheists began holding secret meetings there and in the early years of the nineteenth century plotters gathered in Cecil Court to plan the assassination of George III. Today the alley was the home of Watkins Books, the oldest esoteric bookshop in London, devoted to theosophy, philosophy and spiritualism.

Forrester had known he must come here the moment Arthur Koestler had casually suggested that whoever had been behind the threatening letters to Templar might well have been possessed by some ancient and evil spirit. Forrester did not believe in possession by evil spirits whether ancient or modern, but he was well aware of the power of suggestion, and the manipulation of people of weak mind by those convinced they had occult powers. And if there was one place in London where he could get in touch with such people, it was Watkins Books.

The bell rang cheerily enough as Forrester entered the shop, but the sound was immediately swallowed up by the shelves of magic paraphernalia stretching away into the gloom. A stuffed raven looked beadily down at him from shelves where human skulls broke up the rows of books, and a mandala dangled down from the high ceiling. He paced up and down the shop for a moment, but it appeared to be empty.

"Hello?" said Forrester. "Is anyone here?" Then something prompted him to lean over the counter – and behind it, to his astonishment, he saw a tiny man trying to make himself even smaller, his head covered in a blanket.

"Hello," Forrester repeated, more softly this time. For a moment nothing happened, and then like a tortoise peering out of its shell a head appeared.

"Are you Mr. Smith?" whispered the man, and Forrester could see he was trembling with fear. He was the size of a child, but his features suggested he was in his twenties, and he wore smeary National Health glasses and a ragged jersey. Forrester felt a sudden pity for him, and spoke as gently as he could.

"No, I'm not Mr. Smith," he said. "I'm Dr. Forrester and I've come to see Mr. Watkins. He's an old friend."

"Oh," said the little man. "You haven't come for me?"

"Certainly not," said Forrester, as if speaking to a child. "Why would you think I had?"

"Because of the boots," said the little man. Forrester glanced down at the army boots he had impatiently tugged on that morning.

"He's got big boots like that and you hear them coming after you, clump, clump, clump," said the assistant. "But your head's all right, now I look."

"My head?" asked Forrester.

"They said he's got a funny head. They said I'd die of fright if I saw it, and they'd set him on me if I was bad."

"I see," said Forrester. "Well, I'm not Mr. Smith, and I'm sure you haven't been bad. May I know your name?"

"Oggy," said the little man, "Oggy Pritchard." He held out a slightly grubby hand, and when Forrester solemnly took it, it was like shaking hands with a small bird. "I lost me mam and dad in the Blitz, and I came here to see if I could find them." Seeing Forrester's look of puzzlement, he added, "On the other side, so to speak."

"And did you?" said Forrester, oddly moved by the idea of this poor lost soul reaching fruitlessly out via the occult to parents who had been blasted into infinity by German high explosive.

"No," said Oggy, "but I made myself useful and the Watkinses took me in. I sleep under the counter. Would you like to see?"

And with some pride he showed Forrester an old cupboard drawer which had been lined with an army blanket and provided with a pillow. Primitive though the accommodation was, the bedding was folded neatly and someone had painted on the outside of the drawer OGGY'S BEDROOM: DO NOT DISTURB. Forrester glanced up at the raven and the books of magic.

"Listen," said Forrester, "perhaps you can help me. Someone's been playing a cruel joke on a friend of mine, trying to scare him, make him think a demon is after him, ancient curses, that sort of thing. I was wondering if that person had been buying any books here to gen up on it."

Suddenly Oggy's face was blank. "I don't know nothing about that," he said. "Nothing at all."

"This person would have been interested in very old magic, going right back in time to ancient Sumeria." Oggy remained silent, but Forrester could see the effort that went into it. "Was it the same person who told you about Mr. Smith?" This time the little man's eyes flicked towards the back of the shop – as the office door opened and three men emerged, one a slight scholarly man in his late forties, whom Forrester immediately recognised as Geoffrey Watkins, son of the founder. The second, a Merlin-like figure of about eighty-five with long white hair, was the founder himself, John Watkins, a protégé of Madame Blavatsky – and the third, his massive head shaven and his huge, staring eyes like Mussolini's, was Aleister Crowley.

The self-proclaimed Great Beast, and, for the newspaper-reading public, The Wickedest Man in the World.

Trained in ceremonial magic as a youth by the high priests of an esoteric cult called the Order of the Golden Dawn, Crowley had, according to legend, been recruited by British intelligence to spy on Tsarist Russia. Here his passion for discovering ancient knowledge provided the perfect cover for his espionage, and possibly official protection for his increasingly strange activities, which included founding a religion of his own, the Temple of Thelema, inspired by the Egyptian god Horus, and seducing innumerable men and women with something he called sexual magick.

When details of the Great Beast's practices were revealed in the press he fled to Italy, but even Mussolini's fascists found his goings-on so abhorrent they threw him out.

During the 1930s, Forrester knew, Crowley had spent some time in Norway, where he had recruited Sophie's wayward husband, Count Arnfeldt-Laurvig, in his efforts to summon the devil. There were times when Forrester wondered, in view of the horrors which had descended on Europe afterwards, whether they had not succeeded. Now, ravaged by decades of drug addiction and debauchery, Crowley looked far older than his seventy-odd years, but still armoured by a carapace of voluptuous pride. He walked with the aid of a stick with a curious carved head, and in his other hand he held what Forrester first took for some sort of ceremonial mace. It was a second or two before he realised it was in fact a rolled-up copy of that day's *Evening Standard*.

But he could still make out the headline on the front page: DIPLOMAT MURDERED AT THE BRITISH MUSEUM

Without warning, Crowley placed the newspaper in Forrester's hands and fixed him with his hypnotic eyes.

"A terrible way to die," he said, "at midnight, in the dark, surrounded by ancient idols thirsting for blood."

"How do you know it was midnight?" asked Forrester.

Crowley smiled, as though genuinely amused. "Are you a policeman, hoping to trick me into a confession?" he said. "How funny. But no, the idea of midnight is already there, in the fervid imagination of the journalists."

"I'm not a policeman, and I'm not trying to trick you," said Forrester. "But the man who died was a friend of mine, and I would like to know what happened to him."

"We know this gentleman, Aleister," said the younger Watkins, eager, it seemed, to head off a confrontation. "He's an Oxford man. Do go into the office, Forrester. We'll be with you in a moment."

But Crowley did not seem to want to end the encounter. "Perhaps your friend deserved to die," he said. "Perhaps he had committed sacrilege. Perhaps he had taken something that belonged not to him, but to the gods. The punishment for such crimes is often severe, and dictated by ancient ritual."

"What kind of ritual?" said Forrester, but Crowley was too quick for him.

"If you continue to hope, my friend, that I will reveal some detail of Mr. Templar's murder known only to the murderer, your hopes will, I'm afraid, be dashed. This was a ritual killing, which, sadly, I was unable to witness. But if you ever have the opportunity to see another human being sacrificed on the altar of ancient gods I recommend that you take it. It is a most enlightening experience – and I think you would enjoy it." Suddenly he swung round and fixed his terrifying gaze on Oggy. "Boo!" he said, and with a scream the little man sprang back under the counter and scrambled into his drawer.

Chuckling, Crowley stepped through the open door of the shop and hobbled out into the street.

"I'm surprised you let that swine in the shop," said Forrester.

Geoffrey Watkins swallowed. "He's very hard to say no to," he said.

Under the counter, Oggy whimpered.

7

A CRY FOR HELP

Ten minutes later Forrester was striding along the east side of Trafalgar Square past St. Martin in the Fields, before turning off Whitehall into the redbrick shadows of Great Scotland Yard. In the wake of the morning's assassination attempt on Ernest Bevin, he had expected it to be hard to secure a meeting with Detective Inspector Bell. To his surprise, as soon as he mentioned his name there was a distinct sense of satisfaction from the officer on duty, and he swiftly found himself being escorted up narrow staircases and through labyrinths of dimly lit corridors to Bell's small but oddly cosy office, its walls covered with grainy blown-up photographs of London's most notorious villains.

In short, the room reflected the same energy and purpose that Bell himself exuded. If he had been an East End barrow boy instead of a Scotland Yard detective, thought Forrester, he would quickly have sold everything on his cart. And he was clearly pleased to see Forrester.

"I thought I was going to have to scour the entire city to

find you again, chum," he said, shaking hands. "You seem to be the man of the hour."

"In what way? I thought all anybody here would be thinking about was the Foreign Secretary."

"Panic over on that score," said the detective. "The buggers missed, as you've probably heard; they're on the run and it's a matter of hunting them down. But Mr. Bevin is why we were trying to get hold of you."

"Meaning?" said Forrester, but Bell shook his head.

"All in good time," he said. "While I've got you to myself, I'd like to know what went on when you took Miss Shearer back to her flat. I got the impression from the policewoman who finally came after you that you'd had a bit of a barney there with one of our leading intellectuals."

"That was just the start of it," said Forrester. "I then had a bit of a barney with one of our leading industrialists, followed by a sharp encounter with our premier national practitioner of black magic."

"Let's have it," said Bell, and Forrester told him what had happened since he had left the museum with Templar's wife, including his meeting with Aleister Crowley at Watkins Books.

"I should reprimand you for intruding on police business," said Bell, "but since you've come right round to tell me about it, I'll let it pass." He thought for a moment. "On the other hand, why should a geriatric degenerate like Aleister Crowley want to kill some rising star in the Foreign Office? What has he got to gain?"

"Perhaps that cylinder seal of Templar's has some real

magical significance for him," said Forrester. "Certainly that would explain all the mumbo jumbo about ancient Sumerian curses. It's exactly the sort of nonsense I'd expect Crowley to get up to. By the way, I'm assuming you didn't find the seal on the body?"

"We did not, so the murderer may well have taken it," said Bell. "But unless Crowley's taken some magic potion, I can't see him having the strength to crush the chest of a fit young man like Charles Templar and throw him on the top of an Assyrian statue."

"So he *was* crushed to death? The doctor confirmed that?"

"The ribs weren't just cracked – they were shattered. It was as if somebody had put him in a vice."

"Mr. Smith, perhaps?" said Forrester. "Oggy Pritchard's nemesis?"

Bell pulled a face. "He sounds like just the kind of bogeyman Crowley would invent to frighten the poor soul," he said. "Especially the thing about the big boots." He glanced at Forrester's footwear. "Which aren't all that uncommon, are they? I'll send somebody round to talk to them, but I don't hold out a lot of hope. I've had dealings with those occultists before, and there's nobody better for wasting police time. And then there's this key business." He threw the latest edition of the *Evening Standard* across the desk to Forrester. The subheading read: DID SUMERIAN DEMON PASS THROUGH LOCKED DOORS? beside a picture, clearly taken from the files, of the Assyrian *lamassu* – side by side with a glamour shot of Angela Shearer.

Altogether, thought Forrester, the kind of story for

which an ambitious newspaperman would make a pact with the devil.

"I think the explanation for somebody having an unauthorised key is pretty simple," said Forrester. "They're shifting tons of museum objects back into the galleries from where they were hidden during the war. That's got to involve haulage companies, removals experts, possibly even Army transport units. I'll bet you'll find plenty of extra keys have been cut in the last few months, whatever the keeper of Near Eastern Antiquities said this morning."

"You think he was lying?" said Bell.

"No, I think he was in shock," said Forrester, "and trying to prove he was in control. I bet if you go back and ask him again he'll remember the extra keys." Even as he said this he realised there was another question that should be asked of Horace Darlington. "By the way, you know those photos of the tablets with the threatening messages I gave you this morning?"

Bell rummaged on his desk and pulled out the folder. "I'm not letting you have them back," he said.

"I don't need them back – but it might be a good idea to ask Darlington if he can identify the tablets in the photos. They may even be part of the BM collection."

"You think it might be somebody in the British Museum?"

"I'm not saying that. But if they do have the tablets, are they on display? Could any member of the public have taken a photograph? Or are they in the storerooms, and only scholars can get access? Could help narrow the field."

"Good thinking," said Bell. "But what's bothering me now is how did Templar come to be in the blooming museum at all at midnight?"

"It was midnight, was it? The doctor confirmed that?"

"Then or thereabouts," said Bell. "In fact he says it could have been as early as eleven. But the point is the place was still deserted. Do you think he might have been lured there by whoever was sending him the messages?"

"It seems unlikely," said Forrester. "I know for a fact he was genuinely spooked by them and his nerves had been bad since the war. Even if someone suggested a rendezvous at the British Museum I can't see him just turning up."

"Neither can I. And yet he did turn up – and it cost him his life."

"There is one possible explanation," said Forrester. "He was supposed to collect his wife from the theatre after her show, and of course he never did. She says she went on to a party and left a note for him, and she told me she sometimes sent notes back to the flat when she didn't need him to collect her at the usual time."

"She could be making all that up to establish an alibi."

"She didn't need an alibi: you know as well as I do she couldn't physically have killed Templar in the way he was killed, much less got his body to the top of the *lamassu.*"

"She could have hired someone to do it for her. Or seduced them into it."

"She could, but if she wasn't going to be there herself, why go to all that trouble to create an alibi? No, I think someone faked a note from her to Templar, saying she'd gone to meet someone at the British Museum to put an end to all the threats."

"That would be bloody ridiculous!"

"But it was exactly the kind of impulsive thing she would have done. If someone had said, 'Bring the seal to the back entrance of the British Museum and we'll stop bothering Charles,' she might have fallen for it."

"Even she's not that daft, surely?"

"Maybe not, but Templar might have panicked that she was, and gone haring off there after her."

"Only to find whoever it was waiting for him."

"Exactly."

"So where is this note?"

"In the murderer's pocket, almost certainly. Or a rubbish bin anywhere in Central London. He wouldn't have left it with Templar, anyway."

"It would have needed somebody who could fake Miss Shearer's handwriting."

"It would. But if it's the same chap who's been faking Sumerian curses, I imagine this would be child's play to him."

Bell made a note.

"All right, let's put that to one side for the time being. Did the people at Watkins Books tell you why Crowley had come to see them?"

"Yes, there seems to be some kind of division in the ranks of the occult and he wanted them to help him reimpose his authority."

"There're always divisions in the ranks of the blooming occult," said Bell. "They're constantly falling out and threatening one another, and all too often they come to us and tell on each other. Anything specific this time?"

"Not really. I just got the impression that Crowley has a rival, and that the rival has some source of power Crowley is afraid of, or sceptical about, or both."

"This seal of Templar's?"

"No, not that – I asked them about that and they seemed genuinely mystified. Something else, something more… sinister."

"Oh, God, I've had enough of sinister. Let's talk about Sir Jack."

"Casement?"

"You may have kept the gentlemen of the press away from him for a bit," said Bell, "but they'll be on to his connection with Templar's wife by tomorrow's first editions, so we've got to take him seriously."

"I could hardly avoid seeing that he has a temper," said Forrester, "but there's an element of sheer madness about what happened to Templar, and Jack Casement didn't strike me as a lunatic."

"Oh, he's not a lunatic," said Bell. "If he had been we might have lost the war. The problem is he's not always entirely in control of himself."

"How do you mean?" asked Forrester.

"He was amazingly lucky during the first war, and got out without a scratch. But afterwards, during his barnstorming days, he flew a plane into the entrance of a railway tunnel in Kent and bashed his head in. He appeared to make a full recovery, but every now and then he'll be gripped by such terrible rages people around him fear for their lives. It's all been kept very quiet, partly because he was so vital to the war effort, but the fact is the Yard have had to cover up several nasty incidents. I tell you this in the strictest confidence, Forrester: if you come across him again, watch yourself."

"What sort of things did he get up to?" said Forrester.

"Unprovoked assaults," said Bell. "One on a complete stranger, one on an employee and another on a woman he was involved with. But he apologised, paid all their medical expenses, gave them compensation out of his own pocket and persuaded them not to press charges." Forrester said nothing. "I think if you hadn't steered him away from Angela Shearer's flat today there might have been another nasty incident, this time with the famous Mr. Koestler, who certainly wouldn't have agreed to keep quiet. So you did him a favour there. And you were probably damn lucky yourself."

"So it seems," said Forrester, and thought for a moment. "But Casement had no reason to hate Charles Templar; surely it would have been the other way round, if anything. After all, Templar was the cuckolded husband, Casement the victorious interloper."

"I agree," said Bell. "On the other hand, might he have wanted to get Templar out of the way so he could make the beautiful Miss Shearer his own? The problem is, all this sort of elaborate persecution, the ancient curses and so on and murder in the British Museum, hardly seems his style."

"Unless…" said Forrester.

"Unless what?"

"Unless he was using somebody whose style it was."

Bell looked at him sharply. "Someone acting on his behalf?" he said.

Forrester leaned forward. "Do we know who's been bankrolling Aleister Crowley and his Temple of Thelema recently?"

Bell made another note. "No," he said, "but it's an idea. We'll look into it."

"What about Templar's colleagues at the FO? People like Crispin Priestley and Richard Thornham, who knew all about what was going on. I suppose you've talked to them."

"I have," said Bell, "and a very smooth pair of operatives they are."

"Enough to make you suspicious?"

"I'm suspicious of anybody who had anything to do with this until I can eliminate them. But no, I don't have any particular reason to suspect them: I just react a bit against all that upper-crust blarney. One of them even asked if I was related to the great Gertrude Bell."

"Are you?"

"I've no idea who Gertrude Bell is," said the detective, "so how would I know if I'm related? The point I'm making is they were bloody condescending snobs."

Forrester laughed. "Well that should get them put away for a good long stretch," he said. "Along with the rest of the British establishment."

Bell smiled wryly. "I mustn't be prejudiced," he said, "but since we threw the Tories out I'd begun to think of this as the age of the common man. Half an hour with those blokes in the Foreign Office and I knew I'd been led on."

"Even though a former mineral-water delivery boy is now the Foreign Secretary?" said Forrester.

"Even though," said Bell. "Which brings me to the reason I'm quite pleased you've actually turned up. He wants to see you."

"Who?"

"The Foreign Secretary. *Tout de suite* apparently."

"What on earth for?"

"Search me," said Bell, "but I have a sneaking suspicion it may be something to do with the fact that somebody tried to kill him this morning."

It was only a few minutes' walk from Scotland Yard to the Foreign Office in King Charles Street, yet it seemed as though it was another world. As Forrester stepped inside he was reminded yet again that though Britain was, after the titanic struggle to defeat Hitler, a wounded lion, it was still a lion, with an empire of seven hundred million people.

On the other side of the great Foreign Office doors, immense white columns soared to a gold-leafed ceiling domed like a Byzantine cathedral, each hemisphere thick with richly coloured images of tutelary deities. The whole roof dripped with vast exuberant chandeliers illuminating a magnificent staircase, down which flowed a river of regally purple carpet.

As he went up the stairs, Forrester glanced down into the interior courtyard, virtually an atrium palace of its own, surrounded by the offices from which India was still ruled, however close independence was. No Roman emperor could have asked for a more magnificent seat of government. Indeed, no Roman emperor, even at Rome's apogee, had ever governed so vast a populace.

Nor was the Foreign Secretary's office, when he finally reached it, any disappointment. It was a huge room, full of red leather sofas and highly polished tables, its tall windows looking out over St James's Park and Horse Guards Parade. As Forrester entered he saw the squat, square figure of Ernest Bevin observing this view, his back to him.

"This where Edward Grey was stood in 1914 when 'e said, 'The lamps are going out all over Europe,'" said Bevin. "I sometimes think they're still out."

"I think you're already lighting them, Mr. Bevin," said Forrester. The Foreign Secretary turned, the light flashing off his thick glasses.

"Do you now? Why's that?"

"You're not trying to grind Germany into the ground like they did last time, you're standing up to the Russians, and you've helped set up the United Nations to prevent war breaking out in the future. I think that's a good start."

Bevin nodded. "Well, it's nice to talk to somebody who doesn't think we're getting it all wrong. Most of the time I just get brickbats. And, this morning, bullets. You've 'eard about that?"

"I have. Do you know who it was?"

"My security people tell me it was either Irgun or the Stern Gang. You know much about them?"

Forrester did. Zionist terrorists, sworn to force British troops out of Palestine, had kidnapped and murdered many British soldiers, blown up the King David Hotel in Jerusalem, killing nearly a hundred people, and assassinated Churchill's friend Lord Moyne, the British Resident Minister for the Middle East.

"To my regret I helped train some of them," said Forrester. Bevin sat down at his desk and pushed his glasses down his nose.

"I know," he said. "Tell me about it."

"It was 1941," said Forrester. "Rommel was headed straight for Cairo and it looked as if the Germans were going to push us out of Egypt and take Palestine as well, which would have meant the extermination of every Jew there. Winston decided the SOE should teach the Jewish settlers to wage guerilla warfare, and for a while I did some of the teaching. We were only supposed to be working with Haganah – the Zionist defence force – but I'm pretty damned sure some Stern and Irgun people slipped in as well. They certainly seem to be using SOE methods now."

Britain had controlled Palestine ever since General Allenby's armies, with the aid of Lawrence of Arabia, had taken it from the Turks in 1917. The British government had promised, in the Balfour Declaration, to make it a homeland for the Jews, but a reluctance to offend the Arabs had delayed fulfilment of that promise. For the last seven years both the international Zionist movement and the Jewish settlers in Palestine, known as the Yishuv, had become increasingly impatient. Now, in the wake of Hitler's extermination of six million Jews, the pressure for Britain to act was becoming intense, and groups like the Stern Gang and the Irgun were increasingly turning to violence.

"'Ere's our problem," said Bevin. "We've got to come up with a solution that's fair to the Arabs as well as the Jews. After all, the Arabs 'ave lived in Palestine for as long as the Jews 'ave, and they've 'ad it to themselves for two thousand years. We can't just say, 'Get out, we're giving it to somebody else,' can we?"

"Unfortunately, of course, that's approximately what we've promised to do," said Forrester.

"Well, I never promised it," said Bevin. "That commitment was made thirty years ago by another government. Not that I'm reneging on it, but I'm not going to negotiate under threat of violence. Do you think that's reasonable?"

"I'll be honest with you, Mr. Bevin. I was in Palestine for about eight weeks, I went straight from there back to the Balkans and I haven't given much thought to the Middle East since. But I've got the strongest objections to anybody trying to force our hand by trying to kill you."

"Well, so 'ave I," said the Foreign Secretary, "and that's why I've asked to see you. I 'ad a chat with your new Master while I was in Oxford, and 'e spoke very 'ighly of you, and mentioned you'd worked with some of these people, like you said. Now, I'm going to New York next week for a meeting of this United Nations organisation you're so keen on, and I don't need to tell you New York has more Zionists than Palestine, most of whom seem to 'ate my guts. I'll 'ave all my security people, and all the American security people, looking out for me, but I'd like to 'ave you there as well, because you might recognise somebody that my folk 'aven't 'ad any dealings with. What do you say?"

His eyes met Forrester's as he made the request, and beneath his bluff, no-nonsense manner, Forrester could see the genuine plea in his eyes.

"Yes, of course I'll do it, Mr. Bevin. I'll clear it with the college today."

"Already done. Andrew's fine with it. In fact 'e said it'll kill two birds with one stone, because there's some sort of archaeological conference you want to go to over there and couldn't get the foreign exchange for. Correct?"

"I'd forgotten about that," said Forrester, suddenly suffused by delight, not particularly about the conference but at the prospect of visiting a land which had been part of his mental landscape since he was a boy. There was an absurd explosion of images in his head: of a stagecoach racing across Monument Valley, of Edward G. Robinson staggering, fatally wounded, whispering, "Is this the end of Rico?" and 42nd Street full of dancers.

"Well, that conference'll be your official reason for going there," said Bevin. "I don't want to ruffle feathers by giving you some sort of official position, but you'll be on the boat because you're on the way to this archaeology thing, and I'll get you visitor passes for Flushing Meadows itself. That's where the United Nations is meeting. Toby Lanchester'll give you my itinerary for the rest of the time."

"Toby Lanchester?"

"My security chief – 'e's expecting you in 'is office on the floor above. Don't be surprised if you think it's James Mason."

Before Forrester could respond the door opened and a pretty young woman looked in.

"Mr. Atlee's on the phone, sir."

"Put 'im through," said Bevin, and then stood up and shook hands with Forrester.

"Thanks for stepping in," he said. "I'm sorry to spring it on you, but I don't mind admitting I'm a bit shook up by what 'appened this morning, and I want somebody with a fresh mind. Just watch my back while I'm over in America, and let Lanchester know straight away if you spot anybody you recognise."

He picked up the phone.

"'Ullo, Clem," he said. "What can I do for you?"

Forrester had to suppress a grin as he entered Toby Lanchester's office: he did indeed have the dark, brooding good looks of the man who was at that moment, after box office successes like *The Man in Grey* and *The Wicked Lady*, Britain's favourite film star. But Lanchester was not brooding now; indeed he lay back behind his desk as if he was on a deckchair on a sunlit lawn, wondering whether he could be bothered to ring the bell to ask for more tea.

"My master is very much a believer in belt and braces, isn't he?" he said, looking at Forrester from beneath half-closed lids. "I leave it to you to decide for yourself which of those you are."

Forrester smiled. "Neither, really," he said. "I'm not trained to be part of a security detail and I know there's a risk of me sticking out like a sore thumb. But when Ernest Bevin asks for help immediately after somebody's tried to kill him – well, I could hardly turn him down, could I?"

"No, of course not," said Lanchester. "And I must apologise; I was being rather rude. It's just that I've got rather a lot to think about and your presence will be a complication."

"I understand," said Forrester. "I'll try not to get in your way." Lanchester began to raise his hands in a resigned gesture, and then apparently decided it was too much effort. Forrester began to understand why Bevin might have wanted an addition to his security team.

"I'm sure you'll be awfully tactful," said Lanchester.

"I'll do my best," said Forrester.

"I gather you're from Hull."

"True, though having tact and coming from Hull aren't necessarily incompatible."

"Good Lord," he said apologetically. "I didn't mean to imply that growing up beside the Humber prevented one acquiring *la politesse*. Please forgive me."

"As I understand it," said Forrester, deciding not to be drawn into a discussion of the manners of the inhabitants of the East Riding, "my job is just to keep my eyes open for anybody I know from my time in Palestine, and to pass the information on to you. Is that right?"

Lanchester smiled. "Absolutely right, old chap. The *Queen Mary* leaves Southampton next Monday and I'll have the tickets sent to your college, together with some money for your expenses. As far as anyone else from the Foreign Office is concerned it's just a coincidence you're on the same boat as Mr. Bevin, and the only reason you're going to New York is because of this archaeological conference. The same thing will apply to the American security services: the only two people who will know what you're really doing there are Mr. Bevin and myself. I've arranged for you to stay at the same hotel by the way, the Waldorf Astoria. Will that suit you?"

"It sounds like unaccustomed luxury. I'd been invited to speak at the conference at Columbia and had said no, but perhaps now I can let them know I *will* be available?"

"By all means. The perfect cover. I'll see you at Southampton."

But Forrester was not quite ready to be dismissed.

"Just before I go, I want to make sure you're aware that your late colleague Charles Templar came to me for advice before he was murdered."

"No, I didn't know that. What on earth for?"

"He wanted to talk to me about that cylinder seal someone was demanding he gave back."

"Is ancient Mesopotamia your field?"

"Not particularly. My main area is early Mediterranean civilisation, particularly Minoan. But a friend of Templar's thought I might be able to help him."

Lanchester looked sympathetic. "What a shame you weren't able to. Well, in the sense of saving his life, I mean. What did you tell the poor fellow?"

"What I knew about ancient Mesopotamian mythology.

And what practical steps he should take – including talking to someone like you, which he said he'd already done."

"Indeed he did," said Lanchester. "But sadly all my efforts to help him were as unavailing as yours. Nevertheless, I appreciate you letting me know you'd been involved in the affair."

He turned back to the file, but Forrester persisted.

"So my question is," he said, "is it pure coincidence that Charles Templar was murdered within twenty-four hours of somebody trying to kill Ernest Bevin?"

Lanchester put the file down courteously enough, though his expression was the kind one adopts when speaking to an overenthusiastic child.

"Have you any reason to think they're connected?"

"Not at this stage," said Forrester.

"Still, let's consider it," said Lanchester politely. "Just in case." He steepled his fingers and stared through his window at the rooftops of Whitehall. There was a long pause, and finally Lanchester said, "My initial thoughts are these: almost certainly the people who tried to murder the Foreign Secretary were Jewish terrorists – Irgun or the Stern Gang, probably operating from their Paris base. MI6 has given us plenty of indication this is the kind of thing they're planning and the French Sûreté is notoriously lax about cracking down on them, doubtless because of their guilt in helping the Germans ship so many of them to the gas chambers during the war. Now as you can imagine, their tendency – the Jews, that is, not the French – is to concentrate on one operation at a time; their resources are, after all, limited. This alone, I would say, makes the possibility of a link with Templar's death unlikely. On top of which one has to ask what reason would Jewish terrorists have to kill Charles Templar? His job in the Foreign Office had nothing to do with Middle Eastern affairs, let alone Palestine. And clearly whoever did kill him had some sort of occult agenda; all those threats in ancient Sumerian or whatever it was. I don't think the Jews go in for that sort of thing, however misguided they are. Do you see any Jewish motif in the manner of his death?"

"To be honest I don't," said Forrester, suddenly distracted as he read the title on the spine of one of the books on Lanchester's shelf. It was *The Poetry of Ancient Sumer*, by Edward St. John Townsend.

Lanchester caught his glance. "As you see," he said, "I have given some attention to the question of what happened to poor Templar. But, like you, I have come up with no answers."

"It's the same translation Crispin Priestley used," said Forrester. "The man who helped Templar decipher the photographs that were sent to him."

"Indeed it is," said Lanchester. "Poor Priestley. He's most upset by what's happened, as you can imagine." He rose to his feet, reaching out his hand to shake Forrester's. "Look," he said, "I'm very glad we had this conversation, and I'll make appropriate enquiries, but I have a meeting shortly with the undersecretary."

"Of course," said Forrester.

"See you on the *Queen Mary*," said Lanchester, and dropped back into his seat, as if the farewell had exhausted him.

* * *

The next day saw Forrester back in his rooms at Oxford making the arrangements necessary to cover his academic obligations during the three weeks he expected to be away. In the midst of them, Ken Harrison knocked at the door, his face uncharacteristically grim.

"I'm so sorry I dragged you into this," he said. "You must be feeling rotten."

"Yes," said Forrester. "Templar asked for my help and advice and I was totally useless. I feel as if I've let him down."

"Well, please don't," said Harrison. "Whoever had it in for him was going to kill him whatever you said or did. I should never have got you involved."

"You did it for the best of motives," said Forrester. "Both for him and for me – I know that. But it is a bloody shame."

"Do the police have any idea who did it?" asked Harrison.

"The list of suspects is growing by the hour," said Forrester. He wondered whether he was under any obligation of confidentiality, and decided he wasn't. He'd been giving the police information, rather than the other way round. "Shall I fill you in?"

Harrison sat down and took out his pipe. "I'd be very grateful if you would," he said. "Templar was a good chap and if I can help find out what happened to him, well, frankly, it would be a relief."

So Forrester spent the next half hour describing everything that had happened in London that day, all of which undermined Templar's optimistic assertion that he had no enemies apart from whoever was sending the messages. As Forrester spoke Harrison took out a notepad and began making a list.

"There's no shortage of suspects, is there?" he said at last. "A professional rival or rivals in the Foreign Office, love rivals Arthur Koestler and Jack Casement, possible enemies in the world of black magic such as Aleister Crowley, and of course the beautiful Angela Shearer."

"Who wasn't remotely physically capable of committing the murder herself…" said Forrester.

"But perfectly capable of getting someone else to do it," said Harrison. "We both know that most married people are murdered by their spouse. Perhaps she wanted to get rid of him so she was free to marry Jack Casement. I'm sure Aleister Crowley isn't physically capable of it either, but you've got *him* in the frame, and you have to admit any of the people you've been talking about could have hired somebody to do the deed for them."

"Fair point," said Forrester. "By the way, there's another interesting character associated with Watkins Books: Oggy Pritchard."

"Not another suspect?"

"No, no," said Forrester. "He's a midget who lives under the counter."

"You're joking."

"No, it's literally true. He lost his parents in the Blitz and came there looking for some sort of séance to help him get in touch with them. Geoff Watkins took pity on him and gave him a job and a place to stay. People tend to forget he's even there, so I've asked him to keep his ears open in case he hears anything that might be useful. I mention him in case he tries to get in touch with me here."

"Do you think the Watkins might be working with Crowley?"

Forrester considered. "I talked to both the Watkins after he'd gone and they seemed totally shocked by what had happened and eager to give me any information I wanted." And he summarised what they had told him about the split in the ranks of Crowley's followers and the rumours of a new source of occult power.

"Care to hazard a guess as to what it was?" said Harrison.

"No," said Forrester. "I've genuinely no idea. And I won't be able to investigate any further until I get back from New York."

"New York?" said Harrison.

"Oh, I forgot to tell you," said Forrester. "I've got clearance to go to the archaeology conference at Columbia."

"That's terrific news," said Harrison. "Does that mean you won't need my essay on Athenian shipbuilding till next month?"

"On the contrary, I'm afraid," said Forrester, meeting his eye. "I need you to get it to me by the weekend so that, instead of hearing you read it to me, I'll be able to spend the voyage studying it closely."

8

THE MAN FROM DOWN UNDER

When she was being built in the 1930s the ship was known by the codename 534. The directors of the Cunard Line determined that her name should match those of their existing ships, such as the *Mauritania* and the *Aquitania*, and wanted to call her the *Victoria*, or the *Queen Victoria*, but decided before doing so to ask her grandson's permission. So the chairman of the Cunard board went to see King George and explained that they wanted to christen their new liner with the name of England's greatest queen: to which His Majesty graciously replied, "I'm sure my wife will be delighted."

As a result of which the 534 became the *Queen Mary*.

Forrester could not help smiling to himself at the recollection of this story as he looked up from the Southampton docks at the towering bulk of the liner, repainted from her wartime drabness as a troopship to the self-confident black, white and red of her 1930s glory days. And his mood only improved as he climbed the gangplank and was guided to a first-class cabin by a steward in a white uniform just as crisply perfect as the ship itself.

The first-class cabin, of course, made sense. Bevin would be travelling first class and if Forrester was to keep an eye on him, he had to be in the same part of the ship. For the next five days he would be experiencing a level of luxury he had never known, and he was determined to make the most of it.

He unpacked, delighting in the elegant comfort of his surroundings: the crisp linens, richly varnished woods and gleaming brass porthole, which reminded him of his visits to the trawlers on which his father had worked – although the portholes there tended to be greenish in hue and distinctly reluctant to open. These looked as if they were polished daily to within an inch of their lives. There was even a small writing desk – with two envelopes on it.

The first contained the passenger list, which he put aside to read later. In the second was a note from Roy Bell, brief and to the point.

> "According to Darlington, there are no tablets in the British Museum with inscriptions matching those in the photograph, either on public display or in the vaults, but he kindly gave us a list of other museums to check – a mere dozen or so, in England, France, Germany, Holland, Italy, Cairo and Baghdad. If, having searched them all, the tablets turn out to be in private hands, the keeper said he would be very glad if we could let him know who the owner is so he can set about acquiring them for the museum. Curators! What a bunch! So on

that front we're no further forward.

"I went to see your friend Crowley myself: he's delighted to be a suspect and quite happy to waste as much police time as possible with as many hints and allegations as he can come up with, including the claim that this 'Mr. Smith' is a golem he brought to life himself and can unleash on his enemies at will. He even said, 'You don't have to worry about him now, officer, I've sent him to America.' Absolute tripe, I'm sure, but I felt I should mention it in case you hear the sound of large boots tramping down the corridors of the *Queen Mary*."

Unable to resist the temptation, and as if responding even at a distance to Crowley's will, Forrester glanced at the passenger list. There were four Smiths – one a child, one a single woman, and a couple. To be on the safe side, he decided that when he had time he would check up on the couple, and immediately felt a fool. Smith was obviously a figment of Crowley's warped imagination.

He was about to resume his study of the passenger list when the ship's hooters sounded and he set out along the immaculately carpeted corridors to return to the upper deck.

For the past few years the *Queen Mary* had been anything but immaculate. Painted grey to make her less visible to attacking aircraft, the luxurious art-deco furniture in her staterooms had been replaced with triple-tiered wooden bunks for troops. The swimming pools had been emptied and filled with yet more bunks. Then, relying on her speed to outrun U-boats, the *Queen Mary*, now nicknamed the *Grey Ghost*, had begun carrying as many as sixteen thousand men at a time across the Atlantic to do battle with Hitler's Wehrmacht.

But now, with the war over, all her art-deco magnificence had been restored to the condition it had been when she was launched in 1936. As she pulled away from the dockside, Forrester stood with his hand on her newly scoured rails as passengers threw coloured paper streamers to the crowds below. As he watched, the streamers stretched until they finally broke, and the parting was suddenly real.

He remained by the rail, looking out at the green fields of England as the ship glided down on the Solent, and suddenly felt strangely proprietorial about the land he was leaving. It was absurd, he knew, but having spent five years fighting for England's survival, he felt it somehow belonged to him in a way it never had before he had joined up.

And he still felt protective towards it: to this absurd country with its ruminative farmers ploughing fields their ancestors had tended since before the Norman conquest; its square-towered Saxon churches; its flat-capped working men streaming into their factories in the week and their football stadiums on the weekends; its cheerful, ridiculous Home Service radio comedies (*Can I do you now, sir?*) and sonorous shipping forecasts about barometric pressure falling slowly on the Dogger Bank; its bewigged judges, ermine-clad lords, royal processions in golden carriages; its sweet shops and corner grocers and street urchins yelling out the latest outrageous headlines from its wildly excitable newspapers.

"You love it all, don't you?" said a voice beside him. "The whole ridiculous shebang." And, as he looked down to see Gillian Lytton, for a moment his heart was filled with the same almost unbearable delight he had felt when he looked into the eyes of her sister, dead now these past four years.

"Gilly!" exclaimed Forrester. "What on earth are you doing here?"

"I'm going to the United Nations," said the girl. "To translate for the benighted foreigners. There's a whole gaggle of us aboard."

"That's terrific. I'm so pleased for you."

"And you?"

"Archaeology conference in New York."

"What a bit of luck. We can keep each other company."

"We can," said Forrester promptly, trying to decide how he really felt about Gillian's unexpected appearance.

Gillian was the younger sister of Barbara Lytton, the first woman he had truly loved. Barbara Lytton who, believing Forrester had been killed on one of his missions for the SOE, had volunteered to go to France herself, parachuted behind enemy lines as a radio operator and within weeks had been betrayed, captured by the Gestapo and shot.

Wracked with guilt and loss, Forrester had been unable to deal with the tragedy beyond trying to comfort Barbara's bereaved parents, to whom he had become close. For a long time, amidst his grief, he had felt as if his heart had been permanently cauterised – and then he had met Sophie.

Sophie, whom he had also lost.

The twist to the situation was that he knew perfectly well Gillian Lytton was in love with him. She had had a schoolgirl crush on him when he was going out with

Barbara, and when he met her after the war the feeling had turned to a love he knew he could not accept. His unwitting role in her sister's death placed between him and Gilly, as far as he was concerned, an insuperable barrier. He had told her this, and she had told him not to be so silly. He had tried to stay out of her way, and had largely succeeded.

Now they were trapped together for the next five days. And despite everything, despite the fact that the last thing he needed now was a distraction, despite the fact that he was determined not to hurt her, or hurt himself by opening his heart so soon after losing Sophie Arnfeldt-Laurvig, he had to admit, as he looked at that upturned, open face, that the world seemed a better place.

"I can see you calculating," she said. "Is this embarrassing? Are you here with another woman?"

"Absolutely not," said Forrester. "I'm very happy to see you. Really."

"So you should be," she said. "Unless you're determined to become one of those old bachelor dons."

"To hell with that," said Forrester, suddenly realising that the best way out of his dilemma was to tell her the truth. He knew that his mission was secret, but no one had got around to swearing him to secrecy, and he knew she could keep her own counsel.

"Listen, Gilly," he said. "Let's go for a walk."

And as the great liner left the Solent behind and slipped into the Channel, Forrester walked Gillian Lytton around the deck, explaining exactly what he was doing there and why he could not give her all his attention. As he had expected, she took the situation in her stride.

"It's not a problem at all," she said. "I can be the perfect cover. You can seem to be canoodling with me when you're really eavesdropping on conspirators. And I can be your eyes and ears on the lower decks, which is where all us lowly translators have been stowed. And while I'm with you I can see all the first-class bits."

"I hadn't thought of that."

"Well, I had, and I think it's a terrific wheeze. So will you take me round?"

Forrester did, and for the next hour he felt happier than he had done for months as they explored libraries, beauty salons, music studios, cinemas, lecture halls, paddle tennis courts, and gazed in wonder at the swimming pool hall, two decks tall. They admired the mirrors engraved with eurhythmic ladies, the streamlined bas-reliefs of steam trains being pursued by centaurs and biplanes being chased by winged horses. They looked into the Grand Salon lined with massive pillars which made Forrester think of an art-deco version of the Foreign Office, and drank Buck's Fizz amidst the red leather and gleaming chrome of the Observation Lounge. And then suddenly Gillian looked down the bar over Forrester's shoulder and said, "Isn't that Sir Jack Casement?" which brought the idyll to an abrupt halt.

Forrester had been quite happy to accept Gillian's offer to be his eyes and ears when it was purely theoretical; suddenly the notion that she might come between him and a killer, or at least a potential killer, was distinctly unsettling. And what the hell was the man doing here? Surely if he wanted to go to New York he of all people, as one of Britain's top aircraft manufacturers, would fly? Forrester forced himself not to look round, but Gillian knew from the expression on his face that the sighting of Jack Casement had upset him.

"Perhaps he just likes boats," she said.

"Possibly," said Forrester, keeping his voice low.

"Don't tell me you think he might be here to knock off the Foreign Secretary?" she said.

"No. It's just that he's linked to another case I've been looking into."

Gillian's eyes widened. "Good Lord. I hadn't realised you were turning into a full-time private eye."

"Of course I'm not," said Forrester. "The Ernie Bevin thing is because I was in Palestine during the war. The other business, about Charles Templar, came about because the poor fellow asked my advice about a cylinder seal from Mesopotamia."

"Charles Templar? Oh golly, he's the Sumerian demon man, isn't he? Angie Shearer's husband? The one who was murdered in the British Museum." She looked at him with almost girlish admiration. "You do get the most interesting cases, don't you?" Then her eyes narrowed, just as Barbara's had sometimes done when something puzzled her. "But what does Sir Jack have to do with the demon murder? Don't tell me he was after that cylinder seal?"

Forrester drew a deep breath and realised he had little option but to fill Gillian in on the rest of the story. He was in the middle of it when Casement himself moved along the bar.

"What the hell are you doing here, Forrester?"

Forrester ignored the aggression and explained, politely enough, about the archaeology conference, but Casement's attention was no longer on him. He was looking at Gillian, and when Forrester introduced her, the industrialist immediately enveloped her small hand in his.

"Delighted to meet you," he said. "Let me buy you both a drink." He had to include Forrester in the invitation, but it was clear the only person he was interested in was her. Forrester opened his mouth to give her an excuse to refuse – but Gillian spoke first.

"That's very kind of you, Sir Jack," she said. "We're having Buck's Fizz."

"Possibly, but I'm not giving you any of that muck," said Casement firmly. "The only thing to drink at the start of the voyage is brandy, and needless to say the brandy they serve here is the best."

As he turned to the barman Gillian caught Forrester's eye and pulled a face which said, *Don't worry, leave this to me.*

But the encounter was not going to be as simple as either of them imagined. Even as Casement reached out to sign the bar book an immense paw landed on his shoulder and Forrester looked up to see a huge man with a strong, sunburned face and intelligent, piercing eyes.

"G'day, Jack," said the man. "Fancy meeting you in the lap of luxury."

Casement swung round, and for the first time, for a brief moment, Forrester saw fear in his expression. Then he smiled, showing his surprisingly small, even teeth, and took the man's hand.

"Billy Burke," he said. "Good to see you again."

"That surprises me," said the Australian. "But I'm certainly glad to run into you after all these years." He smiled as he spoke, but the smile came nowhere near his eyes.

"Can I buy you a drink?" asked Casement. "We're having brandy."

"I'll have a beer," said Burke, his steely gaze not leaving Casement's. "For old times' sake."

"So how's business these days, Billy?" said Sir Jack, turning away to the barman.

"Better than it was when I was involved with you, mate."

"Pleased to hear it," said the industrialist. The beer arrived, Burke picked it up in a massive hand and swallowed most of it in one gulp. There was a silence, and Casement, uncharacteristically, seemed to want to fill the gap.

"So what are you up to now?"

"Diplomacy," said the Australian.

"Really?" said Casement, genuinely surprised.

"Fortunes were recouped, donations were made, and a grateful government in Canberra has asked me to go to the United Nations as part of the Australian contingent."

"Congratulations," said Casement.

"Yeah," said Burke. "Your lot haven't sent you as well, have they?"

"No," said Casement. "I'm going to the States on aviation affairs."

"Well, I hope whoever's doing business with you comes out of it better than I did," said Burke, then he put the glass back on the counter with surprising delicacy and walked away.

"These Australians," said Casement, smiling – but his face was pale.

That evening Forrester sat at one of the round tables in the first-class dining room and surveyed his fellow guests. Ernest Bevin and the Foreign Office contingent were two tables away, close enough for Forrester to keep a dutiful eye on them but far enough away for them not to have to acknowledge one another. He recognised the plump outline of Crispin Priestley among the men surrounding Bevin, and there beside him was the tall, thin figure of Richard Thornham, flicking that lock of fair hair from his forehead. Neither of them saw him but he caught a quick, shrewd glance from Toby Lanchester, looking more world-wearily like James Mason than ever.

But no one who looked anything like any of the eager, suntanned young men he had trained in the arts of silent killing back in wartime Palestine – and when he drifted past the table assigned, according to the purser, to Mr. and Mrs. Smith, he saw two benign, elderly white-haired souls who looked as if they should be on the cover of *The Saturday Evening Post*.

Relaxing, he concentrated on the unfathomable delights of the menu, which was replete with such American treats as Seafood Cocktail, Louisiana Coleslaw, Southern-Style Fried chicken, Missouri Beef Brisket and Baked Idaho Potatoes. At the bottom of the menu the Cunard Line claimed, almost unbelievably, that if any guest wanted something not on the menu, they should not hesitate to ask. The red-faced military man sitting beside Forrester noted his expression of astonishment and leaned across confidentially.

"Just to test them a chap from Texas once ordered rattlesnake steaks for four in mid-Atlantic," he said. "And lo and behold they came out with a great heap of roasted eels on a silver platter, with a posse of waiters rattling maracas they'd borrowed from the band. Pretty good show, eh?"

The elegant, horse-faced woman on Forrester's right chimed in. "Our famous British sense of humour. How much it has allowed us to get away with." She offered her hand. "Mrs. Theresa Palmer," she said. "Is this your first crossing?"

Though the woman was at least ten years older, Forrester could not help but be aware of her frankly appraising gaze as she spoke to him. For a fleeting moment he thought how uncomplicated a shipboard romance would be with such a woman, instead of the dangerous minefield he was entering with Gillian Lytton. And then he cursed himself for the thought, and gave an unthinking reply about the archaeology conference in New York, suddenly realising he had more of her attention than he had been bargaining on.

"You study the past," said Theresa Palmer. "I too have a great interest in what has gone before." She fixed Forrester with eyes which were a deep violet and somehow hypnotic.

"In what sense?" Forrester asked, not wanting to know the answer, but feeling strangely compelled to ask.

"In the sense that the past pervades the present, and I want to understand how. I believe there are great patterns in human history, of which we are a part. I believe the study of history can reveal the nature of those patterns."

"I agree," said Forrester, with studied neutrality. "The development of civilisation is a fascinating process." He turned back to the menu.

"I'm not talking about inventing the wheel and writing cuneiform messages on clay tablets, Dr. Forrester. I'm talking about getting in touch with other dimensions."

At the mention of cuneiform tablets Forrester abruptly stopped reading the menu.

"Other dimensions in what sense?" asked Forrester.

"You don't believe we live in a universe of only three dimensions, do you?" said Mrs. Palmer reprovingly.

Forrester smiled. "Four, if you include time."

"Oh, many more than that, my friend. I believe we are like Plato's prisoners in the cave, observing only shadows. That in each of us there are other realities, wrapped one inside another, if only we could see them. That is the true meaning of magick." And from the way she said the word Forrester knew she was spelling it with a "k", as Crowley did.

"Ah," said Forrester. "The occult."

Theresa Palmer smiled forgivingly.

"I see you are not yet a believer," she said, "but even now you should not turn your back on psychic forces."

"Why? Do they threaten me in some way?" He looked at her hard, challenging her. She leant closer.

"I saw you earlier with a lovely girl in the Observation Lounge. And I wonder if I might give you a word of warning."

"What kind of warning?"

"I saw you introduce the girl to Sir Jack Casement. A very sinister aura glows around that man and as I watched it enveloped her too. Hers, when you and she were alone, was bright. As he approached, it dimmed." Forrester's mouth was dry. He strove to remain calm, to not let this woman unnerve him.

"What do you conclude from that, Mrs. Palmer?"

"That she is in danger, Dr. Forrester. That Sir Jack Casement is an evil man, and he wishes her harm. I'm sorry to be so blunt, but I felt it my duty to tell you what I had seen. It's your decision whether or not you believe it." As she spoke she glanced towards the door and when Forrester followed her gaze he was almost certain he saw none other than Aleister Crowley peering into the room. But before he could be sure the door closed and the figure disappeared.

Without thinking Forrester rose to his feet and strode across the dining room and through the door. There was no sign of anyone immediately outside, but Forrester was certain he could hear retreating footsteps on the stairs. He began to descend them, two at a time, holding onto the bannisters to swing himself around the corners.

At each landing, the stairwell was empty.

Then, two decks down he saw a pair of double doors still vibrating on their springed hinges, took a chance, went through them, and saw, twenty yards ahead, a man walking at an unhurried pace past the rows of cabin doors. He paused at one of them and turned to glance casually back at his pursuer.

It was the Australian diplomat, Billy Burke.

He cursed himself for a fool. He had let that woman throw him off balance, distract him. Or had it been more than a distraction? Had she used some sort of mental technique to project the image of Aleister Crowley into his mind as he looked up from the table? Had she deliberately tricked him into leaving the dining room before—

He raced back along the corridor and up the stairs. Several heads turned as he hurried past them, and as he arrived back at the Grand Salon he saw Ernest Bevin and his entourage emerge, unharmed. Bevin himself appeared not to see him, but Richard Thornham did, and registered mild, polite surprise. Priestley's look, on the other hand, was distinctly startled. And then they were past, and Lanchester, behind them, glanced interrogatively at Forrester.

Forrester shook his head, and as he did so remembered, with a sickening feeling, Theresa Palmer's warning about Gillian. He turned to a steward, demanded directions to the tourist-class dining room and found himself pelting along the companionways again, his heart beating wildly till he found the entrance and pushed through it.

And as he looked across the immense room he saw, to his relief, Gillian chatting gaily to a tableful of other young women and let out a long breath of sheer gratitude. But even as he was regaining control of himself a plump, bespectacled young man rose from a table near Gillian's and walked out past Forrester, carrying something in his hand, and the sense of relief vanished as if a cold blast of Arctic air had suddenly blown through the room.

Because the last time Forrester had seen the plump, bespectacled young man was in the Palmach training camp in the mountains of Palestine.

9

THE MAN FROM PALESTINE

He had first met Aubrey Eban when they had both been in Cairo, where the scholarly Jew had been a British army officer charged with censoring Arab letters and newspapers. They had liked each other at once; Eban was a Zionist with a surprisingly strong interest in Arab culture, and he had introduced Forrester to a blind Egyptian novelist called Taha Hussein, who believed Egyptian nationalists should take their inspiration from Greek and Latin culture rather than what he regarded as the sterile Wahhabism of Saudi Arabian Islam. Trapped in his darkness, Hussein was profoundly grateful for the conversation Eban provided, and spending time with Aubrey Eban and this dignified, courtly writer was for Forrester a refreshing change from the cynical, corrupt, alcohol-fuelled atmosphere of Egypt's capital in wartime.

Then, as Rommel's tanks rolled closer and closer to the Suez Canal, Forrester, on Churchill's orders, had been sent to Palestine to train the Jewish settlers in guerilla warfare. Within days Aubrey Eban had been transferred there too in order to liaise between the SOE and the Zionists. Their friendship had continued, but it had been strained as Forrester realised he and Eban had different loyalties. Eban believed passionately that after the war Palestine should become a homeland for all Jews, but Forrester's goals were much simpler. Before anything else could be considered, Hitler had to be defeated.

Eban must have known, Forrester thought, that many of the men who were now England's enemies had been trained in the arts of murder and sabotage during his time as liaison officer. It was very hard for an outsider to know the backgrounds of all the men who attended the SOE courses Forrester had taught, but he was certain that many of them belonged not to the legitimate settler defence groups, but to the Irgun and the Stern Gang.

And now here Eban was, aboard the very ship that was taking Ernest Bevin to New York. As Eban walked away from the dining room, unaware that he had been observed, Forrester went after him.

Eban peered into one room after another – a bar, a library, a smoking room – as if looking for somebody, before finally going through an outer door onto the deck. The night was cold and the ship was rolling harder as it hit the great Atlantic waves, but Eban walked steadily towards the stern, disappearing and reappearing as he passed in and out of the areas illuminated by deck lights.

Forrester tried to see what he had in his hand, and could not.

When Eban finally stopped by the stern rail and peered

out into the darkness, Forrester waited in the shadows for five minutes, and then strode across the deck to stand a few feet away, as if he had come to look down, like his quarry, at the ship's boiling wake. And then he glanced across at Eban, and feigned surprise.

"Aubrey?" he said, tentatively, as though he had just realised this was someone he knew. Eban turned, puzzled. Forrester stuck his hand out. As he did so he saw that what the man had been carrying was a book. "Duncan Forrester. Good to see you again."

"Good God," said Eban, transferring the book to his pocket and taking Forrester's hand in a firm grip. "What are you doing here?" He seemed genuinely pleased to see him.

Forrester explained about the archaeology conference. "And you?"

"I left the army to work for the Jewish Agency," said Eban. The Jewish Agency was the body which officially represented the Yishuv, the Jews already in Palestine, and was charged by the Zionist Congress with trying to establish a Jewish state there. "I'm going to New York to act as the Agency's liaison with the United Nations."

"Do you know Ernie Bevin's here as well, also headed for the UN?"

"I do," said Eban, guardedly.

"I don't imagine you have a very high opinion of him," said Forrester.

Eban met his eye. "Good guess," he said. "Though I certainly don't approve of those who have been trying to assassinate him."

"Who do you think they were?" said Forrester.

"Almost certainly the Stern Gang, and as you know the Jewish Agency has no control over them."

Forrester knew this was true – up to a point. He also knew that the Agency was quite prepared to exploit the results of the terrorists' violence if it brought closer the creation of a Jewish state.

"In my view killing Ernest Bevin would set back your cause by decades," said Forrester. "He's a hero to a lot of people in Britain."

A sudden wave hit the ship, and Forrester had to hold tight onto the rail to avoid cannoning into Eban. Eban touched the book in his pocket as he secured himself with his other hand, and Forrester had a sudden conviction he was waiting for somebody. The deck lights were swinging wildly now, and it was hard to tell if there was someone else out there in the shadows.

"Duncan," said Eban. "It's good to see you again and I remember our time together in Cairo and Jerusalem with great pleasure. The last thing I want to do is quarrel with you, or imply that I in any way approve of anyone trying to assassinate those who oppose us. But I must tell you this: as far as the Jews are concerned Mr. Bevin's behaviour since he became Foreign Secretary has been monstrous."

"Monstrous? Seriously?"

"Britain committed itself to providing a homeland for us in Palestine in 1917. The British Labour Party has voted year after year for that promise to be fulfilled. When Labour came to power two years ago and Ernest Bevin went to the Foreign Office we expected that commitment to be honoured. Instead, the opposite has happened. Hundreds of thousands of Jews who survived in concentration camps are still being kept behind barbed wire in Germany when they are desperate to go to Palestine. When a few of them get out and board some rust-bucket of a ship to run the British blockade they are caught, beaten up and put behind more barbed wire on Cyprus. All this because Bevin does not want to offend the Arabs."

"The Arabs have been living in Palestine since time immemorial," said Forrester. "The Jews left two thousand years ago. It's as if the Italians said they should all be allowed to settle in Britain because the Romans were once here."

"No one has been trying to exterminate the Italians," said Eban. "Within the last decade six million Jews died in the gas chambers. Don't you think the wretched survivors deserve a country of their own?"

Forrester was silent for a few moments. The truth was that since he had seen what the Nazis had done in the concentration camps he had understood all too well the desperation felt by Europe's surviving Jews. But he also knew the kind of difficulties Ernest Bevin was dealing with – and Bevin had asked for his help.

"The problem is, Aubrey, Britain has a mandate to keep order in Palestine between the Jews and the Arabs and Russia's just waiting to exploit anything that goes wrong. Bevin has to weigh all those things up while Irgun and the Stern Gang are murdering British soldiers. Trying to kill him is crazy."

"There I agree with you," said Eban. "I think Menachem Begin and his ilk are dangerous thugs. But what about the kind of Arab leaders Britain has been promoting? Who appointed al-Husseini as Grand Mufti of Jerusalem?"

Amin al-Husseini had become the Grand Mufti in the 1920s, and when in the 1930s Nazi persecution of the Jews led thousands of refugees to flee to Palestine, he had fomented an Arab revolt in which thousands died. During the war he fled to Berlin, and encouraged Hitler in his pursuit of the Final Solution. Now he was busy coordinating Arab resistance to the establishment of a Jewish state.

"I don't know who appointed him," said Forrester. "I assume it was us."

"Specifically, he was the protégé of the wretched St. John Townsend," said Eban. "The great champion of the Arab cause."

"Townsend?" said Forrester. "The chap who translated the Sumerian myths?"

"The same," said Eban. "He's regarded as a hero, a desert scholar, but he constantly championed the rights of the Arabs over the Jews. A perfect example of the kind of man who has far too much influence on the British Foreign Office."

"Where is he now?" said Forrester.

"Last heard of in deepest Arabia," said Eban, "selling oil rights to Stamford Oil on behalf of the Saudi royal family. And as a result of the influence of people like him, Britain has carved seven Arab nations out of the ruins of the Ottoman Empire and is refusing the Jews just one."

"There are some who take the view," said Forrester,

"that it would be better for us to give up the mandate and hand the whole thing over to the United Nations."

"That's exactly what I'm hoping will happen," said Eban. "There's no guarantee the UN will support the idea of a Jewish state either, but I'd rather take our chances there than rely on the British government."

"Good for you, mate," said a voice behind Forrester, and there once again was the huge Australian. "It's all right, cobber," said Billy Burke, putting a massive hand on Forrester's shoulder. "Didn't mean to startle you. Were you looking for me earlier on?"

"I thought you were someone else," said Forrester.

"No," said Burke cheerfully. "I was just me." But his hand remained where it was, and Forrester was acutely conscious of the two-hundred foot drop to the churning wake and the dark waters of the Atlantic. Then the ship rolled again and suddenly only the Australian's grip was keeping him from sliding over the rail. That and the fact that Forrester's right hand was holding firmly to Burke's forearm. He used it to pivot himself to the man's left, and suddenly he was standing a yard away, looking at both men, ready for their next move. They stared at him curiously.

"We should move away from here," Forrester said, forcing himself to keep his voice calm. "I don't think a lifebelt would be much use in that sea."

There was a pause.

"You're right," said Aubrey Eban. "We should go inside."

"Yeah," said Billy Burke. "Why not?"

* * *

They adjourned to one of the lounges, where Burke made it clear he disapproved of British policy in Palestine almost as much as Aubrey Eban did, and as the beers went down revealed that, whatever the Australian government's policy, as far as he was concerned the sooner the Jews got their homeland the better. He also took the opportunity to tell Forrester what a ratbag Jack Casement was, and to explain in some detail how during the Depression Casement had conned him into investing in an aircraft factory just before a major government contract had been cancelled, effectively ruining him.

"If I had my way," he said, "I'd have his guts for garters."

As much to calm him down as anything, Forrester asked where he came from in Australia, and Burke's expression softened. "The Blue Mountains, mate. Great towering cliffs and valleys full of eucalypts and waterfalls. What the Garden of Eden would've been like, if God had had the money. And the echoes! You never heard echoes like them." And suddenly he was declaiming Banjo Paterson's famous lines:

"And down by Kosciusko, where the pine-clad ridges raise

Their torn and rugged battlements on high..."

He took another mouthful of beer.

"The man from Snowy River is a household word today,

And the stockmen tell the story of his ride."

"You should have seen me age ten yelling that from the top of a cliff in the middle of the Bluies and sending model aeroplanes off to ride the thermals. That's where I fell in love with flying." He turned to Forrester and grinned. "If I'd known what a cut-throat business it was building real bloody planes, I'd never have gone into it."

And suddenly Forrester could see before him that bright-eyed outback boy, his planes and his poetry soaring away into the blue, his eyes bright with the promise of the future.

Several people, including Thornham and Priestley, had begun looking their way as the Australian had begun to declaim his poetry and Forrester chose the moment to walk over to where the two Foreign Office men were sitting with an elderly man with a jaundiced complexion and a big blond moon-faced character who couldn't have looked more Dutch if he'd been wearing clogs.

"Forrester, old man," said Priestley. "I didn't expect to see you here."

"Archaeological conference," said Forrester, and trotted out his cover story.

"This is Dr. Nicholas Van Houts," said Thornham, indicating the older man, "formerly governor of Dutch Sumatra, and Jan Loppersum, formerly captain of the tug *Isabella of Ghent*. Now both with the Dutch diplomatic mission to the United Nations."

"Didn't I read something about the *Isabella* during the war?" said Forrester. "Weren't you the people who brought in that wheat ship? The one that was on fire?"

Loppersum looked surprised. "I thought no one remembered that."

"Oh, it was in all the papers while I was home on

leave," said Forrester. "You did a fantastic job."

"There was never any time to read the papers," said Loppersum, shrugging. "As soon as we got back to port, the Admiralty sent us out again."

"Loppersum is a hero," said Nicholas Van Houts. "Everyone in Holland is very proud of him."

"And of the other captains," said Loppersum. "I was only one of many."

Forrester knew just how heroic those Dutch tugboat men had been. They had escaped from Holland with their sturdy little boats as the Germans invaded, and immediately offered their services to the British Navy. Their reward had been possibly one of the most dangerous unarmed naval duties of the war – being sent out among the U-boat packs into the Western Approaches to bring back torpedoed cargo ships that hadn't yet sunk. Scores of badly damaged merchant vessels had been brought into port with much-needed supplies of American food and war materiel because the Dutch tugboats had managed to attach towlines and drag them back. They had saved countless cargoes and crews – but only at immense cost to themselves, because as the convoys vanished over the horizon the slow-moving tugs became prime targets for German U-Boats.

On one of these missions, the crew of the tug *Isabella of Ghent* had gone aboard a blazing freighter they were towing in order to extinguish a ferocious fire in a cargo of wheat, which they had then brought safely home. Forrester discussed the feat for a moment, and then, in politeness, asked Loppersum's older colleague Van Houts about his experiences as the governor of Sumatra before the Japanese invasion.

"It must be infuriating that the Jewish settlers refuse to regard you as their legitimate colonial masters," said Loppersum, and as he glanced across Forrester thought he caught the ghost of a wink. Doubtless his experience as an independent tugboat skipper being ordered about by the Royal Navy had given him a slightly jaundiced view of the British establishment.

"Well, it *is* true," said Priestley, "that the Arabs seem to accord us the kind of respect Jews are reluctant to give."

"You mean the Arabs are suitably deferential, and the Jews stand up for themselves," said Loppersum.

"The Jews," said Thornham, "are a bloody nuisance." He paused as if remembering that he was, after all, a diplomat, and added, "But if I were in their position, I probably would be too."

"Anyway," said Van Houts, "I think Britain would be very wise to hand the predicament over to the United Nations and let the international community sort it out."

"The problem is," said Priestley, "that in the meantime British troops have to hold the ring. And are being murdered daily doing it."

"I bet you wish Colonel Lawrence had never gone to Arabia," said a voice, and Forrester turned to see Gillian. Before any of the diplomats could think of a suitable response, she put her hand on Forrester's arm. "I came to ask if you'll take me to the pictures, Duncan. There's a film I rather want to see."

So Forrester, secretly relieved to be able to slide

away from a conversation which threatened to become acrimonious, took her to one of the ship's cinemas, where they watched a charming new Ealing comedy called *Hue and Cry*, starring Alastair Sim, and for the next eighty minutes Forrester forgot all about Charles Templar, Ernest Bevin and Palestine and sat back to enjoy a light-hearted adventure about stolen fur coats, culminating in a glorious finale where hundreds of children, aided and abetted by an announcer on the BBC, raced from all over London to catch the thieves.

"That was fun," said Gillian as they left.

"Oh, how I loathe adventurous-minded boys," said Forrester in the lugubrious tones of Alastair Sim, and Gillian laughed. She had a lovely laugh.

"Are you allowed to have women in your cabin?" said Gillian.

"Have in what sense?" asked Forrester, and wished he hadn't.

"In any sense you like," said Gillian. "Let's go and see if there are any notices pinned up telling us exactly what we can and can't get up to."

So they did.

As they reached the cabin Forrester glanced down the corridor to see a woman staring at them from the far end. It was Theresa Palmer.

"Are you going to open the door?" said Gillian, and Forrester remembered where he was, turned away from the woman and took out his key.

"Gosh," said Gillian, as the cabin door closed behind

them. "So this is how the other half live."

"You *are* the other half," said Forrester, who had spent time on the Lytton estate at Cranbourne.

"Not anymore," said Gillian. "Land rich and cash poor we are these days, thanks to your crowd." And then she kissed him.

He had been determined to resist, to make it gently clear that he liked her, liked her a lot, but because of the weight of the past they could only be friends. And then he felt the softness of her lips against his and suddenly they were on the sofa, in each other's arms. They sat for a long time, kissing, and then she pulled away from him and looked him in the eyes, and at last shook her head.

"You're not ready yet, are you?" Forrester did not reply. "You're crazy," she said.

"I know."

"It's a self-inflicted wound."

"Not entirely self-inflicted."

"No, not entirely," she acknowledged. "But you don't know what you're turning down."

"I'm not turning anything down. I'm just…" and his voice trailed away. What the hell was he doing? She reached out and touched his face.

"Poor Duncan," she said. "Caught between past and present, like a butterfly on a pin. Poor Gillian, on the same bloody pin."

"You shouldn't be. You're too young and too lovely," said Forrester. "So damn lovely."

"Then do something about it, you fool," said Gillian,

and in answer Forrester leant his forehead against hers and let out a long breath.

"Believe me, Gilly," he said. "I would if I could. But I just bloody well can't." She stood up then, poured herself a drink and sat in one of the armchairs, looking at him over the rim of the glass.

"You remind me of the Isle of Skye," she said.

"Should I be flattered or alarmed?" said Forrester.

"Mummy and Daddy took us up to Scotland one year and we were going to go over there, but there was a deep depression over the Atlantic or something and the sea got up and we couldn't. We just sat there in the car, looking at it over the waves."

"Speed, bonnie boat," said Forrester automatically.

"Like a bird on the wing," said Gillian. "Only we never did. That's why you remind me of Skye." There was a silence while they both thought about the words.

Speed, bonnie boat, like a bird on the wing,
Onward! the sailors cry;
Carry the lad that's born to be King
Over the sea to Skye

"All right," said Gillian at last. "Let's talk about something else. All the murderers, for example."

"The murderers?"

"Well," said Gillian, "all the suspects, anyway. The ship seems to be full of them, doesn't it?"

Forrester laughed. "That depends whether there is any link

between what happened to Charles Templar and what almost happened to Ernie Bevin. Or might happen to Ernie Bevin."

"And is there?"

"I've no idea. Templar worked in the Foreign Office. Ernest Bevin is Foreign Secretary. That's the only link I'm aware of."

"What about the suspects? Are any of them connected to both men?"

"Jack Casement is connected to Templar because he'd been making love to his wife, but apart from the fact that he is on the same boat as Bevin, the link between them isn't obvious."

"Except that during the war Ernie Bevin was providing all the labour for Jack Casement's factories, wasn't he?"

"I hadn't thought of that," said Forrester. "But of course you're right. Bevin was in charge of all civilian workers in Britain during the war, and Casement employed a good many of them. But I've never heard of any conflict between them, and I assume Bevin gave Casement all the workers he needed or we wouldn't have won the war."

"But that doesn't mean that they never clashed, and Sir Jack is famous for his temper."

Forrester thought about what Bell had said at Scotland Yard, about the head injury and the violent outbursts.

"Point taken. But being prone to violent outbursts doesn't seem to square with hiring a bunch of gunmen to shoot up the Foreign Secretary's car."

"Perhaps not, but it seems to fit in awfully well with getting rid of your mistress's husband by killing him in the

British Museum." There was a pause.

"Listen," said Forrester. "I don't want to spook you, but I had an odd conversation with a woman at my table tonight," and he told her about Theresa Palmer and her warning.

"She's a perceptive woman," said Gillian. "Sir Jack certainly did make me feel uncomfortable. I don't know that he wishes me harm, though. Well, depending how you define harm. I've made it pretty clear to him he's barking up the wrong tree."

"Good," said Forrester.

Gillian pulled a face. "Tell me about this Palmer woman. Is she just a concerned onlooker?"

"That's what I've been asking myself," said Forrester, and explained.

"You think she hypnotised you to think you were seeing this Aleister Crowley?"

"Either that or she glanced at the door, thought she saw Crowley herself, and inadvertently put the same thought in my head."

"Why would she think that? Might he be on the ship?"

"I've no idea."

"Have you checked the passenger list?"

"Yes," said Forrester. "And he's not there."

"And you think this woman might be a follower of Aleister Crowley?"

"I don't know that she's a follower. It just flashed into my mind, because of her interest in the occult. But even assuming she is, what would that gang have against the Foreign Secretary?"

"Does Israel play any part in their mythology? Might there be some strange prophecy in the Book of Revelation that they're trying to bring about – or prevent?"

"I hadn't thought of that either," said Forrester.

"Well, it's lucky I'm here then, isn't it?"

He considered for a moment. "Tel Megiddo."

"Tel Megiddo?"

"The real name of the place referred to in the King James version of the Bible as Armageddon. I'm just bringing that up as the kind of thing that might be a link between a bunch of occultists and the future of Palestine."

Gillian's eyes brightened. "So what if Templar had got onto something like that and they did away with him to prevent him passing on what he'd discovered? With the cylinder seal as the clue?"

"Hmmm," said Forrester. "Interesting theory. But it sounds a bit elaborate to me."

"That's only because you didn't come up with it yourself. What about that big Australian? He obviously thinks that Casement did him down in some deal before the war."

"He does," said Forrester, "and if Casement turns up dead before we get to New York I would certainly want to ask Mr. Burke a few questions. But I can't see any connection between him and either the Foreign Office or what happened to Charles Templar." Even as he said these words, however, Forrester realised they weren't true. Billy Burke was now an Australian diplomat and had made his sympathies for the Zionists clear. He was on his way to the United Nations, where the issue would be discussed. And was it coincidence that he had turned up at the stern rail while Forrester was talking to Aubrey Eban?

"All right," said Gillian. "We have to keep him on the list though, don't we? And your pal Aubrey Eban, of course, though when I saw him he looked rather plump and scholarly to be an assassin."

"The odd thing is," said Forrester, "that despite being a passionate believer in carving a homeland for the Jews out of Palestine, he's a great admirer of Arab culture."

"I'm glad to hear it," said Gillian. "There don't seem to be many people like that. What about those two Foreign Office people you were talking to?"

"There's a lot more than two," said Forrester. "Bevin's got an entourage of about fifteen, to say nothing of Lanchester and whatever other security he's brought aboard."

"I mean the ones who were involved with Charles Templar," said Gillian. "The fat one and the thin one who looks like Leslie Howard. Thornberry and Priestman or whatever they're called."

"Richard Thornham and Crispin Priestley. Yes, but I haven't had much time to talk to them in depth," said Forrester, suddenly weary. "I've been too busy dealing with importunate women."

Gillian took an olive out of the bowl on the table beside her and threw it at Forrester, who caught it and ate it.

"You're a bastard," she said.

"Not really," said Forrester. "But I sometimes wish I were."

10

FOG ON THE ATLANTIC RUN

At three pm on Wednesday afternoon, Crispin Priestley stood below the huge wood veneer map of the Atlantic, watching, as a tiny electrically illuminated model of the *Queen Mary* moved almost imperceptibly from east to west along a long groove running through the huge inlaid mural. A stylised moon shone down from the upper left corner of the map and the rays of a golden sun beamed northward from the lower right. The towers and domes of an idealised European city lay over Europe; inlaid images of bridges and skyscrapers glowed on the map of America. Altogether, it was an exhilarating sight, and Priestley seemed absorbed in it.

"They say there's going to be fog," said Forrester, stopping beside him on his way out of the Grand Salon. Priestley started slightly, and then regained his normal sangfroid.

"Not uncommon at this time of year," he said, still concentrating on the little model, "but the Cunards tend to push on through regardless." Apparently satisfied with the progress of the ship, he turned away. "I'll leave you to enjoy the show."

But Forrester fell into step beside him.

"The chap I was drinking with in the bar before I joined you was someone I worked with in Palestine, and I wondered if you'd had dealings with him. Aubrey Eban."

There was a slight pause before Priestley answered.

"Yes, the chap from the Jewish Agency. Clever fellow. But then, they all are, aren't they?"

"All who?"

"The Zionists. And a very tricky lot to deal with, I can tell you."

"I'm sure you could say the same thing about the British."

Priestley smiled. "I'm sure you could. Talking of tricky, by the way, what did you make of poor Charles Templar's death? You must feel badly after he came to you for help."

"I do indeed," said Forrester. "But I don't accept for a moment that there was anything supernatural about it."

"Neither do I," said Priestley promptly. "I believe it was Jack Casement. There's a dangerous fellow if ever there was one. You know he was making love to Templar's wife, don't you?"

"Which would surely be a reason for Templar to kill *him*, not the other way round," said Forrester.

"Logically, yes," said Priestley. "But is murder ever logical?"

"Sometimes," said Richard Thornham, emerging from the library. "In fact, nearly always, in the mind of the murderer. The problem is that murderers' minds are different from ours."

The three of them were now walking together, the ship rolling slightly under their feet as they emerged onto the outer deck. Gradually the air seemed to solidify around them, and Forrester realised the fog was rolling in.

"Different from ours?" said Forrester. "I met plenty of murderers during the war who were just as sane as you and me."

"I'd take that as a compliment," said Thornham, "if I knew exactly how sane you are."

Forrester laughed. "Touché," he said.

"By the way," said Thornham, "I must congratulate you on that very pretty girl who asked you to take her to the pictures. She seemed rather smitten."

"She's the sister of someone I knew in the war."

"Well, in that case I'd say you were a very lucky fellow," said Thornham. "And speaking of women, had you heard it needed a hundred and twenty female French polishers to restore the woodwork on this fine ship after the GIs had finished carving their initials into it?"

"I had not," said Forrester, "but I am duly impressed."

"And do you know how many different types of veneer there are on board?" said Priestley.

"So far I've been lucky enough to avoid that kind of conversation," said Forrester.

"Well your luck has run out," said Thornham, "because Priestley has them off by heart."

"Ash," said Priestley. "Beech, cherry burr…"

"Cedar, for the cigar room..." put in Thornham.

"Tiger oak," added Priestley.

"Pear wood," said Thornham. "Ceylonese satinwood..."

"Sycamore," got in Priestley.

"And lemonwood," Thornham concluded triumphantly.

"Well," said Forrester, determined not to be distracted by the double act, "I'm eternally in your debt – but I wonder if either of you know an Australian diplomat called William Burke, commonly known as Billy. He's with us too, and seems to be an old enemy of Sir Jack Casement as a result of some business deal that went wrong."

"Then he's in good company," said Thornham. "There are plenty of people who'd like nothing better, after doing business with him, than to push Sir Jack Casement off the back of the boat."

"I was telling Forrester," said Priestley, "that Casement is my number one suspect for doing in poor old Charles Templar."

"Why, because he wants to marry his wife?" said Thornham.

"Exactly," said Priestley.

"Well, she is a bit of a stunner," said Thornham. "But you'd have thought Casement could have arranged a separation between the two without murdering the husband in the depths of the British Museum. Surely even the trickiest divorce court proceedings would have been simpler?"

"Unless all that supernatural malarkey was designed to throw us off the track," said Priestley.

"Oh, I don't think so," said Thornham cheerfully. "My money's on the Sumerian demon."

At which point the ship's horns began to hoot mournfully an octave below middle A and suddenly the fog was impenetrable.

Near the rail, the vapour glowed from within where it clustered around the deck lights, like clumps of spiritualist ectoplasm in which other passengers appeared and disappeared as if they themselves were ghosts. Forrester turned to the two veneer experts and found they had vanished. Then James Mason materialised through the fog, and it was a second or two before Forrester was close enough to see it was only Toby Lanchester.

"During the war she ran down one of her own escorts in a fog like this," Lanchester was saying to the man beside him. "She cut the escort in two, but had to steam on because of U-boats, leaving hundreds of poor chaps in the water to die."

"I heard that Churchill was aboard," said the other man, "under the name of Colonel Warden."

"I trust your charge is safely tucked away in his suite?" said Forrester.

"I wish he was," said Lanchester, "but he's playing gin rummy with the Aga Khan." And then the fog swallowed him up.

"I heard that twelve thousand GI brides went to America on the *Queen Mary* last year," said a woman's voice. "Isn't that romantic?" But before Forrester could identify the speaker she had vanished. Then Forrester saw Billy Burke in conversation with – he was almost certain – Richard

Thornham. He moved towards them – as Casement passed by, inches away but apparently oblivious to his presence. Then the military man from Forrester's table was beside him.

"She nearly rolled completely over one night in forty-three," the colonel was saying. "Sixteen thousand GIs aboard. They were in a gale seven hundred miles from Scotland when a rogue wave hit them. One moment the top deck was at the normal height and then, whoosh, she was rolling right into the ocean. They say if she'd gone another three degrees over she'd never have righted herself."

"Duncan?" said another, lighter voice: Gillian. Damn! What was she doing out here? He'd thought she was safely inside with some of the other girls from the UN.

"Over here," called Forrester, peering into the mist.

"Duncan!" said the voice again, with more urgency, but further away.

"Gillian!" said Forrester. "I'm right here."

"Where are you?" came her voice from the far side of the deck now, but it might have been from the far side of the world. She sounded scared. His stomach knotted, Forrester strode towards where the sound appeared to be coming from.

"Dr. Forrester!" said a woman's voice, and Forrester saw Theresa Palmer, droplets of moisture gathered in her hair. "You must go to her at once." And then she too was gone. Without warning his way was barred by a bulkhead and his fingers were wrapping themselves around the cold metal stanchions of a ladder. Unthinking, he began to climb it, his feet slipping on the moisture-laden steps. And then he was on an upper deck, with the lifeboats directly above his head.

"Duncan!" came a faint voice from ahead, and he began to run, blindly, the foghorn deafening him, the massive funnels rising like prehistoric monuments into the greyness on his left. And then his feet were on an oil slick and shooting out from under him and he was face down, sliding helplessly along the smooth, wet wood.

Straight toward the rail.

As he reached it a hand came out of the mist, slid out the restraining pin that held the hinged section in place, and swung the gate open. For a split second he was plunging straight down at the churning sea two hundred feet below, and then his right foot caught on a metal upright and he jerked to a halt, hanging upside down over the water.

For a moment he was simply too stunned by the speed of events to take action, and then a boot slammed into his ankle. It was a big boot, an army boot, and he cried out in pain, and his assailant kicked again, so hard he seemed to feel the bones crack, and he knew that any second now he would be dislodged, and he'd be swallowed forever in the darkness of the Atlantic.

With every ounce of his will he ignored the pain and jack-knifed himself upwards, grasping the lowest of the rail's wires with his left hand. Freeing his agonised foot from the stanchion and hanging there, he looked up at the monstrously misshapen head looming above him in the fog as his assailant moved far enough back to kick Forrester's fingers agonisingly into the wire.

For a moment Forrester felt an atavistic fear, before his rational mind forced him to recognise that his attacker had simply pulled a burlap sack over his head and was looking at him through a slit in the material. Fighting down the pain, Forrester brought his right hand up to grasp the stanchion on the far side of the gap before his left lost its grip. Then he hauled himself higher and as his head came up the man's knee slammed into his face, sending him swinging away from the rail again, his vision blurring, blood pouring from his nose, with a single hand keeping him from falling away into the waves.

It was then that the knife came out and Forrester cried out uselessly as it sliced down towards his fingers. He tried to swing himself back towards the rail and found the momentum of the ship made it impossible. This was it, then. The blade would sever every tendon and he would fall and never know who had done it to him.

And then, in mid-descent, the knife stopped, and Forrester was looking at Gillian, white-faced, as she swung the deckchair at the sack-hidden head and the wood splintered against it and the big boots were thudding away down the deck and the man was gone. She reached out her hand to pull him back in.

"Oh, God," said Gillian Lytton. "I thought I was going to lose you."

It had been neatly done, Forrester had to admit, and beautifully simple. Olive oil, taken from one of the dining rooms and poured onto the deck by whomever he had been lured into following, at the exact place a fall would bring him closest to a hinged section of the rail. If it had all gone according to plan, if Gillian had not seen and followed him, he would have vanished into the Atlantic and never been seen again.

"Whoever did it," said Forrester, staunching the blood flowing from his nose. "They're good."

"Shut up," said Gillian, all her fear turning, without warning, to fury, "it's not a bloody game. He was going to kill you." And suddenly she was in his arms, sobbing against his chest as the fog swirled around them. As he held her, Forrester suddenly remembered the terrified little man in Watkins Books, talking about Aleister Crowley's mythical creature, Mr. Smith. Mr. Smith of the big boots and the misshapen head.

Had he been aboard the *Queen Mary* with them all along, waiting for his chance?

"You look as if you've been through a meat-grinder," said Gillian. "Let's get you to the doctor." But at that moment the ship's alarm bells began to ring, the rhythm of the engines changed dramatically, and over the loudspeakers came the announcement:

"Would all passengers please return to their cabins, and all crew report to their mustering stations. Please be assured there is no danger to the ship, but we have a man overboard."

The *Queen Mary* turned then, and for several hours criss-crossed the sea along the path it had been taking, but no one was found. During the rest of the night stewards searched the public rooms and visited each cabin, checking the passengers off on a long list. It was only at breakfast the following morning that word went round that the lost man had been identified.

It was Billy Burke, of the Australian diplomatic mission to the United Nations. He would never again, thought Forrester, see his beloved Blue Mountains, or watch his model aeroplanes ride the thermals to the words of "The Man from Snowy River".

11

NEW YORK, NEW YORK

Two days later the *Queen Mary* approached The Narrows emitting a thin sliver of steam from her funnels. She had picked the pilot up at Sandy Hook, together with a detective from the New York City Police. Even while the search for Burke had been going on Forrester had briefed the Foreign Office security man on the attempt to kill him, and Lanchester had listened intently.

"But you couldn't identify him?"

"He had a sack over his head, but I'd recognise those damn boots if I saw them again. And the knife too."

"I'm quite certain the sack, the knife and the boots went overboard within minutes of him failing to kill you," said Lanchester.

"Or perhaps of him succeeding in killing Billy Burke," said Forrester.

"If it was the same man."

"You know there was bad blood between Burke and Jack Casement, don't you?" said Forrester.

Lanchester shook his head decisively. "I'm quite certain Jack Casement has nothing to do with this," he said. "He's got bigger fish to fry than some tuppence-ha'penny Australian."

"How do you mean?"

"Jack Casement is now Britain's biggest aircraft manufacturer. Without the planes he makes, our trade balance would be about twenty per cent worse than it is, and he's come here to make deals to sell more. We're not going to let anything get in the way of that."

"Unless he's a murderer."

"I'm telling you, he's not a murderer. He had no reason to attack you, and Mr. William Burke probably drank too much beer, as Australians tend to do, and fell off the back of the boat. No, what happened to you has to do with the fact that you're here to help protect Ernest Bevin, it's as simple as that."

"I'm not sure it is," said Forrester.

"Well, I am," said Lanchester decisively. "Whoever has it in for Mr. Bevin has spotted you and decided to get rid of you because you found something out, something that could help identify him. And the question is, what?"

And for the next half an hour he and Forrester compiled a list of pretty much every encounter he had had since he came on board, including the brief glimpses of people in the fog before he had been lured onto the upper deck. Together, they cross-questioned the purser and his staff, but none of them had seen anything useful, or anyone resembling either Smith or Crowley. As they left the purser's office, Lanchester lowered his voice.

"Listen, Forrester, I'd like you to keep quiet about both this attack on you and the animosity between Jack Casement and Burke. The captain is sure to have reported Burke's disappearance to the authorities in New York, which is why the detective is aboard, and if he talks to you I want to make sure he has no reason to think there's any connection between you and the Foreign Secretary or Billy Burke and Jack Casement."

"Why not?"

"Because whatever they say about confidentiality, if the New York police know about it, the American press will find out too, and there's enough bad feeling in New York about Mr. Bevin without giving them a lot of sensational guff."

"You mean Palestine?"

"New York's full of Jews and the newspapers are all on their side," said Lanchester. "Let's not give any more grist to their mill with talk of Aleister Crowley and his imaginary bogeymen. Or cramp Jack Casement's style by having him dogged by a lot of false accusations. The country needs him to do deals for us, Forrester. Don't get in the way of that."

Forrester found himself on the back foot with Detective Terence O'Connell the minute he limped into the cabin the detective was using for his interviews. O'Connell reminded Forrester irresistibly of a New York fireplug, but a smart, shrewd and observant fireplug.

"Trip over something?" he said, looking at Forrester's swollen nose.

"Bar stool," said Forrester.

O'Connell nodded. "Tough break," he said. "And how did you hurt your hand?"

Forrester smiled wryly. "Trying to stop myself from hitting the floor," he said. "And I promise you, the three whiskies had nothing to do with it."

O'Connell did not smile. "Bourbon?" he said, and Forrester cursed himself for making the elementary mistake. Don't elaborate. Never provide more details than they demand. "The whiskey you were drinking, was it bourbon?"

"Johnnie Walker," said Forrester, smoothly enough, but he was certain O'Connell had seen the microsecond of uncertainty in his eyes as he came up with the answer. He thought he was on safer ground as he answered the questions about the archaeology conference and his reason for visiting New York, but he had failed to take account of the fact that when a story hit the papers in London it didn't stay in London.

"I heard about that thing at the British Museum," said O'Connell. "That guy being offed by some kind of demon. That must have had all you archaeologists in a tizzy."

Forrester forced himself to smile easily. "It would have done if the newspapers had got it right," he said. "But it was all nonsense, just journalists getting carried away."

"Which you know because…?" said O'Connell, and Forrester realised the detective had lured him neatly into another trap. He decided to play the stuffy academic.

"Because I am a historian, Detective O'Connell, not Edgar Rice Burroughs. I know about ancient Mesopotamian mythology, but that's all it is, mythology. I've no idea who killed Charles Templar or why, but I can tell you the supernatural had nothing to do with it, because the supernatural does not exist."

"Yeah, it's lucky nobody believes in that stuff anymore," said O'Connell, "otherwise you'd have people going to church at Easter and claiming to believe in the Resurrection. But I guess you Oxford guys are beyond all that."

Damn, thought Forrester, *this man is smart*. Again he took refuge in pomposity.

"Not believing in long-dead religions doesn't prevent a person from being a Christian," he said.

"Okay," said O'Connell, "that's a relief. You had me going there for a minute." And then he started in on his questions, which made Forrester feel like a stuntman in a movie doing battle with the finest swordsman in France. The NYPD had not sent their most easygoing detective out to the *Queen Mary*, not by a long chalk. How much time had Forrester spent with Burke during the crossing? Had he had any arguments with him? Had he seen anyone arguing with anybody else? Where had he been when the ship sailed into the fog? How well did he know Sir Jack Casement?

It was, therefore, with some relief that he finally limped out of the temporary interview room and out onto the deck, where Gillian was waiting for him in the sunshine, and he was in time to see one of the greatest sights of his life.

Ahead of them was the Statue of Liberty, her torch aloft, an image he had seen so many times in pictures that seeing it in reality was like a hope fulfilled.

On either side of them, in the harbour, were freighters, battleships, tugboats, ferryboats, fireboats, lighters, launches. Beyond them rose the skyscrapers of New York, glittering with confidence and prosperity, effortlessly proclaiming this narrow island as the new capital of the world. Forrester had left behind a London battered into poverty, a Paris humiliated by defeat and occupation, a Rome discredited by its own foolishness, a Berlin that had been justly smashed to smithereens by those it had tried to destroy. The old order was reeling – here was the new.

When the great liner sounded her foghorn the sound echoed off miles of waterfront from which the products of American industry poured out into the world, echoed again off Wall Street towers where the world's most important financial decisions were made, off garment district sweatshops where the world's fashions were created, and Broadway skyscrapers where the world's music was plinked and tinkled into being. To Forrester it seemed as if the entire island of Manhattan was surging out of the water like a whale propelled by its own sheer exuberance.

Gillian squeezed his hand. "This is fun, isn't it?" she said. "I'm so glad I'm seeing it with you." And Forrester couldn't help agreeing. This was one of life's great moments, and Gillian was the perfect person to share it with. And then the image of Sophie's face came into his mind, and Barbara's, and he had to force himself to stay in the moment. And managed it, almost.

To do otherwise would have been letting the side down.

* * *

Engines stilled, the *Queen Mary* was guided onto Pier 90, the hawsers were secured to the bollards, the gangplanks lowered and people began to stream through passport control towards the customs sheds. As Forrester watched O'Connell leave, he wondered how far his investigation had taken him: between boarding the ship and its arrival in New York he seemed to have interviewed at least twenty people – and from the expression on his face Forrester guessed he hadn't got anything definitive. Nobody, at any rate, was being detained.

Ernest Bevin made a brief statement to the press saying how pleased he was to be here and how much he was looking forward to discussing international problems with the whole international community at the United Nations. The statement was punctuated by the crackle of flash bulbs, and followed by a volley of disregarded questions, before a fleet of Town Cars spirited the Foreign Secretary and his team to the Waldorf Astoria. Forrester was staying there too, but knew discretion required he arrived there separately, and concentrated on seeing Gillian onto the bus that was waiting to take her and her fellow translators to the hostel near the General Assembly building on Long Island.

The tanneries and slaughterhouses of Turtle Bay were already being demolished for the permanent headquarters of the United Nations, but it would be years before that would be completed and in the meantime the organisation designed to secure the peace of the world was housed in an old gyroscope factory at Lake Success and a former ice-skating rink at Flushing Meadows, where the 1939 World's Fair had taken place. Gillian held him tight before she got onto the bus, and told him to be careful, and he promised to come out to see her as soon as he was able. As he did so he knew he wasn't just being polite: he needed to see her. He needed to talk to her again. He needed to hold her.

He watched the bus for a long time as it was swallowed up by the city and then saw, among the crowds, Theresa Palmer getting into a limousine. As if sensing he was looking at her, she raised her head and looked directly into his eyes before the car door closed behind her. There was a voice behind him.

"I'm staying at the Paramount Hotel on Broadway. Come and have a drink if you get a chance." It was Aubrey Eban. "Or catch up with me at the UN. If you have time from your archaeology conference, it should be worth a visit." Then a man in a leather windcheater came towards them and guided Eban towards a waiting van. As the van pulled away, and Forrester was walking towards the ranks of exuberant yellow taxis, a Cadillac cruised up beside him.

"Want a lift?"

He glanced into the dimness. It was Jack Casement. For a moment he hesitated, and then knew that, whatever the risks, this was an invitation he had to accept.

"Thanks," he said, and got in.

Forrester glanced across the car towards the industrialist, his face light and dark as shafts of sunlight slanted down through the girders of the elevated railway above their heads. "ROOMS, $1.50" said a sign on a building amidst a dense tangle of fire escape ladders. "BUDWEISER PREFERRED EVERYWHERE." "ADMIRAL TELEVISION APPLIANCES." "GIANT TWO-TROUSER SUIT SALE."

"This is very kind of you," said Forrester.

"It's not kind at all," said Casement. "It's the perfect opportunity to tell you to get out of my hair."

Forrester blinked. "I beg your pardon?"

"I don't appreciate being followed, Forrester," said Casement. "I didn't appreciate it in London, I didn't appreciate it on the *Queen Mary*, and by God I won't put up with it in New York."

"I wasn't following you in London, and the only reason I was on the boat is that was how I was getting here for the archaeology conference."

"Travelling first class? I know academic budgets. It's not your college picking up the tab, is it?" It was a shrewd thrust, and Forrester knew he had to take control of the conversation.

"So who do you imagine is paying for it, Sir Jack? Somebody who believes you killed Charles Templar?"

Casement looked genuinely surprised. "Who says I killed Charles Templar? Why would I kill Charles Templar?"

"Perhaps because you wanted to marry his wife."

"I was making love to his wife. That doesn't mean I want to marry her."

"So who did kill him?"

"I've no idea. Any more than I know who killed Billy Burke." Forrester saw the tiny flicker of uncertainty in

Casement's eyes as he realised those last words had been a mistake.

"I thought he was supposed to have fallen off the back of the boat," said Forrester.

"He probably did, judging from the amount he drank."

"But you just said he had been killed. And there was bad blood between you, wasn't there? He told me you'd tricked him into investing in an aviation company you were planning to abandon. Nearly ruined him, he said. Did you have an argument? Did he slip and fall?"

Suddenly Casement was angry, his hands clenched into fists.

"I didn't kill Billy Burke and I didn't kill Charles Templar, but I bloody well *will* kill you if you don't tell me who put you up to this."

Through the window behind Casement, Forrester saw they did not seem to be driving direct to the centre of the city but were going through a part of town which seemed to consist of nothing but abattoirs. There were carcasses hanging in the wide openings, carts full of offal, blood in the gutters and the stench of death. His eyes flickered towards the bullet-headed chauffeur driving the car: this was shaping up to be an ambush.

"Nobody 'put me up to this'," said Forrester. "But somebody tried to kill me on the *Queen Mary* and damn near succeeded. From the way you're talking now I'm beginning to wonder if it was you."

The industrialist tapped on the glass and the car stopped. Two men pushing a cart loaded with carcasses paused beside